DISCOVERED ESCAPE

DISCOVERED ESCAPE

JULIE BAWDEN DAVIS

Roses
A R E
RED
PUBLISHING

Cover by Judy Bullard (customebookcovers.com)

Book design by Julie Bawden-Davis

Palm logo design by Kayla Curry

Roses are Red logo design by Kyle Kane

ISBN 13: 978-1-955265-37-9

ISBN 10: 1-955265-37-2

Distributed by Roses Are Red Publishing

rosesareredpublishing.com

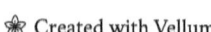 Created with Vellum

ACKNOWLEDGMENTS

As they say, it takes a village. Here's my village. I'm supremely grateful to each of these fabulous people!

ARC Reading Gems
Julie Schlueter
Tara Bradley
Susa Fraccaroli
Kery Bailey
Trish Darrenkamp
Marilyn Smith
Lisa Starkey
Beth Helm
Chelle Young
Jacquelyn Gray
Penny McCulloch
Ellen White
Karen McTyeire
Heather Wamboldt
MelK
Amber Mancebo

Pros
Sharon Whatley, editing
Judy Bullard, cover design
Kyle Kane, logo design
Sabrina Wildermuth, design consultation
Jeremy Davis, technical support

To those separated from loved ones.

PROLOGUE

ONE WEEK EARLIER

Patrick Tomlinson got the call just before midnight. He set down the book he'd been reading and answered.

"Yeah?"

"It's time."

"When?"

"The process begins now. You take care of this, it'll all be over."

"I want a guarantee."

The man on the other end of the line took slow, even breaths, then replied, "There will be a sign for you to look for. A yellow rose."

Patrick switched the phone to the other ear. "What?"

"You'll understand when you encounter it."

He stared up at the roughhewn wooden ceiling of his small cabin. He was so tired of the games, the endless codes, the doublespeak. And of so many years spent alone. "You're telling me a flower is my guarantee of freedom? Do you know how bat-shit crazy this sounds?"

"Await further instructions. They will arrive shortly."

"That's all I've been doing is waiting—for almost ten

years," Patrick said, his irritation rising. "Hello?" But the caller was gone.

He went to a window and pulled back the curtains to peer out into the dark night of the Puerto Vallarta jungle surrounding his cabin. Was this finally his chance to regain his life? He thought about his mother, brother, and sister. Especially Cherie. He'd done everything, including disappear, to protect them.

He sensed movement outside. Grabbing the handgun he kept in the kitchen drawer, he moved quickly to the door, then leaned against it and listened. Above the constant hum of the insects in the jungle, he heard the crackling sound of footsteps on the path. He turned the knob and pulled the door open, ready to shoot, but there was no one anywhere in sight. Then he heard the low rev of an engine and a car driving away.

Patrick was about to go back inside when he noticed a small, white box at his feet. After picking it up with one hand, he shut the screen and dead bolted the door. Then he took the neatly wrapped parcel to the kitchen and set his gun on the counter. Putting the package to his ear, he listened. Silent.

He took out a boxcutter and began to open the missive. Was this the last piece of information he needed?

1

Patrick shut the door to his cabin and locked it, then hoisted on his backpack. He placed his hand on the doorknob in a silent goodbye. He had called this little cabin in the jungle home for the last several years. He wasn't sure when he'd be coming back, if at all.

Dressed in dark pants and a T-shirt, his hiking boots on, he made his way down the narrow road surrounded by tropical forest, the sound of insects buzzing around him in the otherwise still night air. When he'd first gotten here, the hum had annoyed him, but now the sound comforted him—like one small thing he could count on. He neared the end of the drive and thought about his sister, Cherie, and her recent visit, then quelled the feelings of hope that he'd learned to smash down over the years. He had more to do before he could regain his old life, if that was even possible. All he knew was the next few days were out of his control, and wherever this journey took him, it was the only way out.

He eased his backpack off and set it on the road. Pulling his cellphone out of his pocket, he checked the screen. Five minutes until three am. He was early, but that was planned.

His contact had made it clear. Be on time or his ride would keep on driving.

He wondered what Cherie was doing now. He'd gotten into the habit of doing that—picturing his family going about their days, imagining what those days looked like. Cherie dressing for work at the FBI, Tad with his nose buried in a book at college, Mom finishing a shift at the hospital. Just then, he saw headlights flashing in and out of the dense jungle terrain as a car made its way toward Patrick. He slid his phone into his pocket.

When the vehicle was several yards away, the lights flashed off and on several times. He grabbed his backpack and walked toward the car as feelings of tension and anticipation rolled around in his belly. What was expected of him in the coming days appeared impossible.

A Range Rover pulled to his side of the road and the passenger window lowered. Patrick could see an older man, a day's stubble on his face, his bald head shining in the dim interior light. "You ready, Tomlinson?" asked the man.

Patrick gave a nod and headed for the passenger seat.

"Put your pack in the back," he said.

Patrick did as instructed, then climbed in and slammed the door.

The man eyed Patrick carefully, then jutted out a hand. "Monte Arroyo. I've heard good things." The man had a vice-like handshake.

"I'd like to say the same, but this is the first I've heard of you," admitted Patrick.

The man laughed, a deep rumble in his chest. "To the point. I like that." He shifted the car into drive and headed out onto the road. "The fact that you haven't heard my name is good. I try to keep it that way."

Patrick smiled. He could relate.

Monte glanced over. "I'm not sure how much they told you about our destination."

"It's my understanding we're going to Veracruz so I can get some training."

Monte took a cigarette out of a packet on his dashboard and stuck it into his mouth but didn't light it. He nodded. "Make yourself comfortable. We've got a thirteen-hour drive ahead of us."

Relaxing was going to be hard now that Patrick was closer than he'd ever been to going home to Jersey. The will to return was so strong he could almost taste and smell and feel it, and when things got this visceral for Patrick, he knew that he was about to step into something.

"Patrick, doll, come on in. Frankie isn't here, but you can wait for him," said Suzette, a leggy brunette dressed in a short, black skirt and skintight tank top studded in rhinestones. Patrick knew she worked at the strip club downtown, but since he was only seventeen, he'd never been there. He looked down, afraid he was staring.

He sat on the edge of the couch and waited, sneaking glances as Suzette poured herself some whiskey, then swirled the liquid around in the glass and downed it. He could smell her perfume across the room. When she finished, she turned to him and smiled. "I'd offer you something to drink, but I know Frankie wants you fresh for the job." Her eyes swept Patrick as they often did, then came to settle on his face. She leaned against Frankie's mini bar. "You seem like a nice kid. What are you doing here?"

Patrick took a deep breath just as Frankie Mariano burst in, two of his crew members behind him. He was stocky, with a heavy jowl, generous stomach, and slicked back, dark hair. A cross of rubies hung from a gold chain around his neck. On his left pinky finger was a gold ring encrusted in diamonds in the shape of a triangle that Patrick had heard scarred the faces of many men.

"There you are," he said to Patrick, then brought his attention to Suzette. "What the hell you doing standing around in your show getup? Put some clothes on. I don't need the kid with a hard-on."

Suzette rolled her eyes and stalked off to the back of the apartment.

Frankie snorted, then turned to Patrick. "Go to the gas station's convenience store like we talked about and take photos with the camera Nick gave you." He pulled out a fold of cash from his back pocket and handed it to Patrick. "If the guy gives you any trouble about the photos, tell him you're working on a school project or something."

Patrick put the money in his pocket.

Frankie clamped down on Patrick's shoulders with his beefy hands and spoke, his breath a pungent mix of garlic and beer, "You got this kid. You hear?" Then Frankie let go of Patrick. "Drop the camera off when you're done. Give it to Broderick." Frankie pointed to one of his men. "He'll be answering the door tonight."

2

They turned toward their destination the next day just as the sun was setting, the sky ablaze with orange and golden light. Patrick saw a small house built of wood and stone set against the Veracruz mountains. The property was nestled in the midst of palm tree groves, and he spied several small sheds behind the house. A child stood barefoot next to the driveway holding a chicken in her arms.

Patrick and Monte got out of the car, and the child squealed, "*Tío* Monte! Look at my chicken, Luciana!"

Patrick waited as Monte approached the little girl and said, "Are we having her for dinner, Violetta?"

"No, *Tío*!" Her eyes grew wide. "She lays eggs."

The man chuckled. "Okay, if she lays me some eggs, I won't try to eat her." He reached into his pocket and took out a shiny coin, pressing it into the little girl's palm. She began jumping up and down, the chicken's feathers flapping.

"Where's *Tío* Estevan?" Monte asked her.

"In the house. I have to put Luciana to bed in the chicken coop." She headed toward the back of the property.

Monte turned to Patrick. "Estevan has been out of the

business for a while. You're fortunate he offered to train you. He's a man of few words, so listen when he does speak, because those words are gold."

Patrick nodded, then followed Monte up the steps and through the front door, past a small entryway into a homey living room, where a man stood to greet them. Even dressed simply in a T-shirt and jeans, he was imposing.

"Estevan," said Monte as the two embraced. "You're looking well, and so is Violetta. I didn't see Loretta."

"She's gone to the store. She'll be back soon."

The two men turned to Patrick then, and Monte introduced him. "We really appreciate you taking him on," he said to Estevan.

Patrick stood still, keeping Estevan's gaze as the man sized him up. Estevan said, "I agreed to this with the understanding that no trouble will come knocking on my door."

Patrick started to speak, but Monte put up a hand. "You've got our word. Just an even exchange for your fee. Then Patrick will be on his way."

Estevan held out his hand and Patrick took it. As they shook, he could feel a solid strength and calm in the man before him.

"Welcome to our home," said Estevan. He gestured to an armchair. "Would either of you like something to drink? *Cerveza?*"

"I've unfortunately got to go," said Monte, who remained standing. "Tell Loretta I'm sorry I missed her. I'll come back for a long weekend when I can." He turned to Patrick. "You're in good hands."

Once he left, Patrick said, "If I could have a glass of water, that would be great."

Estevan went to the adjoining kitchen and filled a glass from the spigot and handed it to him. Then he sat down while Patrick took a long drink. When Patrick finished and

Estevan didn't say anything, he asked, "It looks like you grow palm trees here?"

Estevan relaxed back in his armchair. "Yes, palms for the local markets. There has been a lot of construction up and down the coast, and the palms are popular."

"How long have you been farming palms?"

"For decades. This was my father's farm. Before I married, I also worked for a number of years for *La Causa*, the organization that fights injustice and is helping you. That work often took me away from the palm tree farm, but nowadays I stay close."

"And that's why you've agreed to train me? Your work with *La Causa*?"

Estevan leaned forward and folded his hands, looking down at them, then at Patrick. "I agreed to train you after reading about the special circumstances surrounding your situation. In particular, your efforts to reunite with your family. The child you met outside, Violetta, is my niece. My sister and her husband were killed in crossfire due to a cartel altercation."

"I'm sorry to hear that," said Patrick.

Estevan nodded just as a woman walked in the front door. Patrick stood as his host made two long strides to the doorway to greet her. He gave her a kiss on the cheek and took a sack from her arms.

"I got everything," she said, then turned to Patrick, who approached and extended his hand. The woman's face lit up in a bright smile. "This must be our guest for the week. I'm Loretta, Estevan's wife."

"I appreciate you hosting me," said Patrick, taking her hand, which was soft yet confident. "I'm Patrick."

"We're happy to have you. You'll spend the days here, but since our accommodations are limited, we'll be putting you up just down the lane at our neighbor's house."

"I'm grateful for whatever accommodations you can provide," said Patrick.

"How about I take you to Sonrisa's to get settled now," said Loretta.

Patrick turned to Estevan. "When would you like me tomorrow?"

"At sunrise. Meet me in front of the house."

Patrick followed Loretta down the driveway and along a pathway lined with brush. The sun had set now, the way lit by what remained of the daylight. "Where are you coming from?" she asked him as they walked.

"A little cabin in Puerto Vallarta," replied Patrick.

"You must miss your home. I hope you will feel welcome here during your stay."

They came to a small house then, a curl of smoke rising from the chimney in the early spring air. Patrick smelled an enticing aroma.

"I would have fed you dinner," said Loretta as they headed for the set of steps leading to the front door. "But Sonrisa's cooking is so much better than mine."

"It sure smells delicious," said Patrick as they stood on the small porch.

"Sonrisa," Loretta called out through an open window.

Footsteps clamored inside, and the door whipped open, a boy of about eleven stood in the entryway. Grinning, he unlatched the screen door and opened it for them. They walked inside, the interior of the house much different than Patrick anticipated. The walls were covered with dynamic, colorful paintings using different mediums, and the floor comprised a pattern of hand-painted tiles in shades of purple and jade.

"Where's your mother, Juan?" Loretta asked the boy, who wore shorts and a T-shirt, his feet bare.

"Out back."

Loretta turned to Patrick and smiled. "Sonrisa is an artist —a very accomplished one."

"This is her work?" he asked.

"Isn't it beautiful? She sells it at a gallery in downtown Veracruz."

"And I sell my mom's tie-dyed T-shirts at the farmers market," said Juan, standing straighter as he spoke.

"Something smells yummy," said Loretta.

At that, Juan cried, "The chili!" He rushed toward the back of the house.

Loretta laughed, and they followed him to the kitchen, where Juan vigorously stirred a pot on the stove.

The back door opened then, and in stepped a woman. She wore her long, blonde hair pushed back by a purple bandana, and the front of her yellow smock was splotched with multiple colors of paint. She stood in the door frame, her pretty, violet-blue eyes direct as she met Patrick's gaze. He tried to pull his eyes from hers but couldn't. Instead, he waited for her to speak. He thought he may have murmured hello, but he couldn't be sure. The moment unnerved him.

3

Sonrisa Herrera knew her guest would soon arrive. She had reluctantly agreed to host someone because Estevan had done so much for her. After hanging the shirts she had just tie-dyed on the line and rinsing her hands, she went through the back door to find Loretta and a man standing in the kitchen. He was tall and fit, with chiseled features, and such a penetrating look she had to glance away.

"Sonrisa, this is Patrick, our visitor," said Loretta.

Sonrisa focused on wiping her wet hands on the front of her smock, then met the man's eyes again.

He gave her a warm smile and said, "You have a great home here. I find your art especially intriguing."

His compliment seemed genuine. "Thank you. Some people think it's a bit much."

"I think it's just right," Patrick said.

"Well, it looks like you're off to a great start," said Loretta. "I'm going to head home. Let us know if you need anything at all."

When Loretta left, Sonrisa glanced over at Juan to see him busily stirring the chili, most likely to mush. "That's good, Juan. Go ahead and turn off the stove, and how about setting the table?"

"I'd be happy to help," said Patrick.

"That's okay," Sonrisa started, but Juan pointed above his head. "The chili bowls are on the top shelf."

"Juan." Sonrisa shook her head.

Patrick smiled and reached up and pulled down three bowls and set them on the table. "Have you always been an artist?" he asked Sonrisa as she took off her splattered apron and hung it by the back door.

"Since I was young."

"My mom won awards for her art," said Juan proudly as he plunked the pot of chili on the table, then began ladling some into the bowls.

"That was a long time ago," said Sonrisa. She pulled open a drawer and took out some cloth napkins, handing one to Patrick and then Juan.

Patrick unfolded his napkin. It was one of Sonrisa's favorites, ice-dyed with swirls of different colored blues. He studied it. "This napkin is beautiful. Your work, too?"

"Yes, thank you," said Sonrisa. "Would you like something to drink? I have some beer."

"A beer would be great," said Patrick, folding the napkin to lay on the table.

"I'll take one," said Juan.

Sonrisa chuckled, took two beers out of the refrigerator, then grabbed a glass and jug of milk and set that in front of Juan.

Patrick took a bite of his chili, nodding approvingly. "Thank you so much for your hospitality."

"Did you come far?" asked Sonrisa before taking her first bite of chili. She was curious to know more about this man.

"From Puerto Vallarta," said Patrick.

"You live there?"

Patrick seemed to consider her words for a moment before responding. "For the last few years." He took some tortilla chips from a bowl on the table and broke several over his chili, then glanced over at Sonrisa. "How about you? How long have you been here?"

Sonrisa felt the familiar tug of anxiety at the question. Then she reminded herself that Estevan had sanctioned Patrick's visit. "Juan and I have been here for ten years," she said, bracing herself for the next question that always came.

"And before that? You're American?"

Sonrisa swallowed a mouthful of chili and washed it down with a drink of beer. "Yes. You?"

Patrick wiped his mouth with the napkin. "Me, too. Nice to meet a fellow expat."

Sonrisa thought about asking him where in the States he was from, but she didn't want to open up the dialogue. That would only lead to more questions. Instead, she changed the subject. "We've got brownies for dessert."

"I love brownies," said Patrick.

"Not more than me," cried Juan.

Patrick was enjoying this. He'd been alone for so long and eaten each meal by himself, he'd forgotten how nice it was to sit down with other people. Not to mention that he found Sonrisa particularly appealing. He wanted to ask her more questions, but then he'd have to answer the same. Instead, he decided to enjoy the good food and good company.

"What do you do for fun?" he asked Juan.

"I like to fish," the boy said. "And I want to hunt rabbits, but my mom won't let me use a rifle."

"Fishing is good. What do you catch?"

"Big, big marlin," said Juan, setting down his spoon and spreading his arms wide.

Patrick laughed at his enthusiasm. "That is a big fish. Who prepares the fish?"

"Estevan showed me how to cut it up," he said proudly. "My mom doesn't like that part, but she does cook it really good."

"It can be pretty messy to clean a fish," said Patrick.

"And smelly," exclaimed Juan, who had finished his chili. "Can I have a brownie now, Mom?"

"If you stop talking about smelly fish, yes. Then you need to get your schoolwork done."

After Juan was excused, Sonrisa got up and said, "You'll be sleeping in the sunroom. I'm afraid it's not much."

"I'm sure it'll be perfect," said Patrick as he followed her out of the kitchen to a small room off the living room. There was a futon and chest of drawers, and shelving lined with pottery.

"The room fills with sunlight in the morning. If you'd like, I can cover the windows."

"Estevan wants me at his place at sunrise, so this is fine."

Sonrisa glanced around the room, then back into Patrick's eyes. "Well, then, I'll let you get settled."

She started to turn when Patrick said, "Wait."

As she looked at him, he saw anxiety on her face.

"I just wanted to say thank you. I really appreciate you taking me in."

Sonrisa's tense expression relaxed. "You're welcome. I owe a great deal to Estevan. I'm happy to help him."

"I'm afraid to ask, but I need to," said Patrick's mother. "Where did this money come from?"

Patrick had just given her five hundred dollars toward the mortgage. "I told you. It's from my job at the yogurt shop."

"You make minimum wage there."

"I've been working extra hours."

His mother slid out of her nursing shoes and wearily rubbed one foot. "But you're sixteen, Patrick. You should be focusing on school, not working so many hours."

"You needed the money, right?" asked Patrick, the irritation he felt creeping into his tone. "Would it be better if we lost the house and had to live on the street?"

His mother's eyes softened, and she reached out and took his arm. "I didn't mean to sound ungrateful. I just worry about you. You've taken on so much responsibility since your father's been gone."

Patrick felt bad for getting angry with his mother. It wasn't her fault Dad had died fighting in Afghanistan. Patrick knew, as the oldest, it was up to him to help keep a roof over their heads. And Patrick was going to do just that.

4

Patrick woke the next morning just before the sun came up and slipped out of Sonrisa's house. At this pre-dawn hour, it felt refreshingly cool outside. He knew that once the sun rose, the day would warm up considerably.

While he headed to Estevan's, he recalled last night's meal with Sonrisa and Juan. He enjoyed how easy and companiable the experience had been. Silly jokes and laughter around the dinner table—that was something he had dearly missed over the last several years.

"Patrick, where were you?" asked his sister, Cherie. It was early morning on a school day, and he had just gotten home after an exhausting night running "errands" for Frankie. She looked at him, head tilted, hands on hips.

"Studying late with Sherry. I fell asleep at her house." A rift of guilt passed through him, and he immediately wished he could confess what he'd really been up to.

His kid sister was smart. She knew when he wasn't being truthful. He could tell by the expression on her face. She didn't call him out on it, though, but changed the subject instead. "I'm going to wake up Tad, then make his breakfast. You want me to make you some eggs? Mom came home from the hospital a little while ago and went to bed."

"I'll get myself something," said Patrick. "You just take care of Tad."

Patrick watched his sister go down the hall and soon heard her talking in low tones to his younger brother. He went into the kitchen and poured himself a large mug of coffee and stood there waiting for it to cool down. Patrick hated being dishonest with his mom and sister, but telling them he was working for a New Jersey mob wouldn't go over too well. Besides, the gangsters in this part of the country were notorious for going after family members as retribution. He wasn't about to test them. The thought of what could go wrong terrified him. He downed half of his mug of coffee at once. It was the only thing that would get him through the school day.

Walking up the drive to Estevan's, Patrick jumped when the man stepped from the shadows. "Lesson one," Estevan said quietly. "Attuning your hearing. It's critical that you hear everything. I could have sunk a blade into your belly before you even blinked."

Patrick grimaced and glanced at the still dark sky. "Is that why you wanted me here before daybreak? To listen to the night sounds."

"That's part of it," said Estevan. "Close your eyes and tell me what you hear. Not the sounds, but what you hear."

Patrick shut his eyes and listened intently. He heard a swoosh as a breeze lifted the grass surrounding them, and then a dry rustling sound, maybe leaves falling. In the distance in the surrounding jungle, he heard a whisper, a faint swish. The movement was nearly imperceptible.

"I hear the grass moving in the wind, and dew pattering to the ground. I also hear a small animal moving through the nearby brush, maybe a woodchuck or a rabbit."

"Good," said Estevan. "Now I want you to walk toward the jungle with your eyes closed. The land is flat here, with no obstructions, so you'll be fine. Listen as you go and stop before you are a few feet from the edge of the jungle. Then tell me what you experienced, not just what you heard."

Patrick closed his eyes, this time turning to face the tropical forest. He slowly moved toward it. As he did so, he felt the breeze on his face, then suddenly recalled the sound of sirens. He stopped short. "Sorry, I'm not sure why, but memories are coming up."

"That can occur, but whatever happened in the past needs to stay in the past," said Estevan. "I have read your file, and I know a good part of what you experienced. That has no bearing on the here and now. Do you understand?" The man's voice was firm but not harsh.

Patrick took a lungful of air, steadying himself. "I do, yes." He squeezed his eyes closed and kept walking.

Sonrisa had woken at the sound of her guest leaving at dawn. She lay in the still house gazing up at the ceiling shrouded in the dark and wondered about his adventure. What was Estevan training him for? Sonrisa knew little about Estevan's work. She had heard in town once that he worked for powerful men, but for good. How he had helped her since she came to Mexico was an indication of that.

She stretched, then sat up and glanced at her bedside clock. If she hurried, she could work on her current painting before Juan got up for school. She pulled open her bureau and took out a plain, cotton dress and changed, then made her way to the kitchen and put coffee on to brew. In the sunroom, she found that her guest had neatly made his bed. His backpack leaned up against the wall, and there were no other items left out. She went over to the pack and took a closer look. It was stuffed to capacity. She tested the weight. Heavy. Then she decided to stop snooping and went back to the kitchen to pour herself a giant mug of coffee with three spoonful's of sugar.

In her studio, Sonrisa turned on the overhead light and stood before her canvas—a scene from her old life. The Golden Gate Bridge at sunset. When they relocated her here ten years ago, she was warned against putting too much of her old life into her paintings, but she found that including bits and pieces of her past soothed her. And the Golden Gate Bridge was so iconic. She had captured that five-minute period when day melted into colorful streaks of topaz, with a touch of purple, as night took over.

The owner of the art gallery where Sonrisa showed her

work liked it when she included people in her paintings, so for this scene she had added pedestrians and cars on the bridge. Some people were walking, while others had stopped to look out over the bay. She cast the water below with refracted light, sparkles bouncing off the surface. Then Sonrisa looked at the cityscape she had painted in the background and thought, would she ever be able to return home?

5

"The scent of fear can be picked up several yards away," Estevan said. "You never want anyone or anything to smell fear on you."

The two men stood in the jungle, the air warming as night transformed to day. Patrick had just finished practicing standing perfectly still for long periods of time, hands shoved deep in his pockets to steady himself.

"Let's get something to eat," said Estevan, starting toward the house.

When they were in the kitchen, the house still quiet, Estevan reached into a basket of eggs sitting on the side-board and cracked several into a hot pan with oil. He then filled two mugs with black coffee and set them on the table. After piling plates with eggs and getting out forks, he sat down across from Patrick.

Patrick took a sip of coffee, then said, "Thank you. For everything."

Estevan met Patrick's eyes. "I've been where you're at. My father was killed when I was fifteen, so not much older than you when your father was killed. My father taught me much of what I am teaching you now, and though your father died thousands of miles away, he taught you by his example."

Patrick nodded and waited.

"There are times in our lives when we have a choice. We can fight for those we hold dear, or we can cower and take the easy way out, which in truth becomes the hard way. You have already combatted and won against fear by standing up to wrongdoing and protecting your family. Remind yourself of that when your way becomes challenging. Now eat before your eggs get cold."

"Mom," said Juan, nearly causing Sonrisa to drop her palette of paints. "The bus will be here soon."

Juan stood in the doorway of her studio fully dressed, a paper sack in his hands, his backpack on.

"You're ready for school?" she asked, surprised, glancing at his hand. "Is that your lunch? You could have told me. I would have helped you."

"You looked really busy with your painting," said Juan. "I didn't want to bother you."

Sonrisa heard the bus lumbering down the road and set down her paints. "Let's get you to the bus."

As they headed down the front steps, she asked, "Please tell me you made yourself something nutritious for lunch."

When Juan didn't answer, she laughed. "You can tell me after school." She gave him a brief hug, careful not to embarrass him in front of the other children watching from the bus windows. Jorge, the driver, gave her a quick wave before he pulled the door shut. Juan and Violetta lived farthest from the school. It was a long drive, but Jorge came for them. Sonrisa suspected it was Estevan's influence.

She turned toward the house when she spotted Patrick and Estevan heading into the jungle carrying shotguns. An uncomfortable feeling overcame her. She knew they would just be doing target practice, but the sound of gunfire made her feel like scratching her way out of a cardboard box. She hurried back into her art studio and turned on her favorite CD, "Brahms Violin Concerto," to the highest reasonable level. Then she squirted some paint on her palette and got to work.

After lunch, Estevan left to do some errands with Loretta, and Patrick headed back to Sonrisa's. As he got closer, he heard loud classical music. He wondered if she was working on her art. He had never known a professional artist but had always been fascinated by the process. How artists came up with ideas, then somehow executed those ideas intrigued him. When he got to the stairs, he hesitated, unsure of what to do. It wasn't like he could knock and be heard, and he didn't want to alarm her. He stood outside the house for some time, then finally decided to enter.

Sonrisa had the door open to her studio, and her back to the doorway. Patrick stopped several feet away to watch her work. He saw an undeniable rhythm to the way she painted. Several brushstrokes, then she cocked her head and studied what she'd done, then the paintbrush went to the palette and she began working on another portion of the painting. He could see she was painting the Golden Gate Bridge. He had never been to San Francisco but recognized the bridge from photos. She was working on the cityscape beyond the arches of the bridge. Patrick took a few steps forward.

Her heart freezing, Sonrisa spun around and met Patrick's eyes. She looked down to see that she had spattered paint across her feet and on the floor. He approached, his hands in the air. He was saying something, but she couldn't make out what over the music. She set her palette and brush down and went to shut off the CD.

"I'm really sorry," he said. "I didn't mean to frighten you."

Sonrisa balled her hands into fists to stop her arms from shaking.

Patrick noticed the paint on the floor and moved closer. "Let me help you clean that up."

Sonrisa said louder than she had intended, "No, it's okay."

Patrick stopped at her tone and nodded slightly. "I feel responsible."

"It's my fault," she said. "I shouldn't have had the music up so loud."

Patrick looked at her canvas. "The Golden Gate Bridge at sunset, right?"

"Yes," she said, then changed the subject. "If you want something to eat, help yourself in the kitchen."

"I ate with Estevan but thank you." He hesitated, then

backed out of the room. "I'll let you get back to work. I've taken too much of your time already."

Sonrisa nodded as he walked out, then shut the door. She wet a rag and began dabbing up the paint from the floor, glancing up at the painting as she did so. Maybe it was time to start another one.

6

Patrick went into the kitchen to pour himself a drink of water, confused about his exchange with Sonrisa. He'd seen her trembling, as if his entrance had more than frightened her, but instead had terrorized her. He wondered again about her circumstances as he looked out at the swing set and firepit in the backyard. He glanced around the kitchen, noting a corner of the counter stacked with earthenware mugs that looked handmade and spice bottles lined up in front of a colorful mosaic backsplash. The place had an inviting, artistic feel, and yet something about the house felt unsettled. As if a feeling of stability was missing—a sense of belonging never having taken hold. Patrick noticed it because it was the same feeling at his house in Puerto Vallarta.

Sonrisa's studio door opened then, and she came into the kitchen. "Forgive my rudeness," she said. "My reaction was uncalled for. I'm not used to anyone besides Juan being here, and since he's at school, you startled me."

"It's alright," said Patrick. "I might have had the same reaction if I were surprised. I'm sorry about my being here. I can see that it's throwing off your routine. I should be out of here in a few days."

Sonrisa studied him for a moment. "Would you like a cup of tea? I have an herbal mix that I make myself with chamomile and lemon rind."

"I'd love to try something you made yourself," said Patrick. "You continue to impress me."

He noticed a small smile turn up the corners of her mouth as she put the kettle on to boil. "You flatter me," she said.

"It's true. No sense denying it," Patrick said.

As they waited for the water to boil, Sonrisa pointed at the back door. "If you want to sit outside, I can bring the tea to you."

Out of the kitchen window, Sonrisa watched Patrick give the empty swing in the backyard a push, then he sat down in a lounge chair. He had an easy, quiet way about him that Sonrisa liked. She also appreciated how he spoke with Juan at the dinner table last night. He treated her son like Estevan did—with respect, and he didn't talk down to him.

The teakettle began squealing then. She shut it off and pulled out an earthenware jar containing tea grounds. Then she put a couple of heaping tablespoons into the kettle and grabbed two mugs and carried it all outside to set on the table between two lounge chairs. She went back inside and returned with a small crock of honey. When she opened the door, Patrick jumped up and reached out his hand for the honeypot. "The tea has a terrific fragrance," he said.

"This is one of our local honeys," said Sonrisa as she handed him the pot. "We can sweeten our tea with it."

She sat beside him, settling her skirt around her ankles, leather huaraches on her feet. Sonrisa loved this time of the afternoon when a lazy, relaxed feeling settled in the warm air. She breathed in a small, contented breath.

Once they were sipping their tea, Sonrisa asked the question she had been wanting to ask. "How long have you been in Mexico?"

Patrick hesitated for a moment, then his shoulders relaxed, and he sighed. "Nine years. I'm working on making my way home." He seemed grateful for her interest, but she imagined he had to tread lightly. Too much information was always a danger, she thought.

"This training that Estevan is giving you. Will it help you return home?"

Patrick turned to her, a troubled expression in his eyes. "I hope so."

Sonrisa lifted her mug toward Patrick's. "Well, then, I also hope so for you."

It was a week later that Patrick came back one evening after being with Estevan and announced that his training was complete. Sonrisa couldn't help but feel disappointed. Even though she'd known this was temporary, she looked forward to the dinners, and their lively conversations. With Juan telling his outrageous stories from school, and Patrick adding his own tales from when he was young, the three of them would sit at the table talking well after they finished their meal.

"You'll be going then?" asked Sonrisa, for want of something to say.

Patrick frowned and said, "Yes, tomorrow morning early."

He glanced at the table, set with dinner. Sonrisa and Juan had made *arroz con pollo*. "Smells delicious as always," he said.

Sonrisa had a sense that Patrick was somehow comforted by their time together, and Juan's animated chatter always made him laugh. She wondered if he was going to miss them.

She glanced over at Juan, who held a notebook in his hand. He'd been drawing and wanted to show Patrick. By the expression on her son's face, she could tell he was also feeling sad at the news. To break the mood, she clapped her hands together and exclaimed, "Tonight we will celebrate you finishing your work with Estevan. Perhaps he, Loretta, and Violetta would like to join us for dinner. We have plenty."

"I'm sorry, I meant to tell you earlier," Patrick said. "Loretta asked me to convey the news. Her mother was admitted to the hospital earlier today. They are heading out tonight for the States. She said she will contact you once they know what is happening."

"Oh, I'm so sorry to hear that. Loretta's mother is a lovely woman. She hasn't felt well for a while. It will be just us then. Juan, how about after dinner you make your apple crepes."

Juan seemed to brighten at his mother's request, and the mention of dessert.

It was nearly midnight when Sonrisa yawned. She and Patrick had sat outside talking under the stars after Juan had gone to bed. Though they tiptoed around each other's backgrounds, they discovered that they both had a love of astronomy. Patrick pointed out several planets and a constellation. Sonrisa wasn't exactly sure what else they talked about. She just knew she enjoyed Patrick's company. The evenings would seem empty without him, the days longer.

When they both stood to head inside for the night, Sonrisa tripped on the edge of her skirt and Patrick reached out to steady her. She laughed then, feeling clumsy, Patrick's hand firm on her arm.

"You okay?" he asked, his voice thick.

Sonrisa felt a heat rise in her from his touch and gave her skirt a well-defined shake as if that might somehow rid her of her emotions. Patrick exuded strength, warmth, and a smell that said all male. Her heart quickening, she decided to stay quiet, rather than appear foolish. When he took a step toward her, hand still on her arm, and it seemed as if he might kiss her, Juan suddenly appeared in the doorway. Patrick let go of her, and she turned to her son. "Juan, what are you doing out of bed?"

"I heard a weird noise out front of the house."

"Probably just an animal," she said. "Go back to bed."

"I'll go check," said Patrick.

Juan went back inside, and Sonrisa said to Patrick, "Thank you." Then she followed Juan in. Though she was thankful for Patrick's reassurance, the possibility of someone being outside unnerved her. She went into the kitchen to wait.

Patrick stole to the front of the house, putting to use all that Estevan had taught him over the last week. He pushed himself up against the wall and held his breath when he heard the imperceptible sound of crackling brush. As he stayed quiet, he wondered if anyone besides Estevan and Loretta lived close. He stood deep in the shadows for some time, listening silently for more movement. Finally, he went around to the back of the house and tapped on the door.

Sonrisa opened it quickly and let him in. She had turned off all the lights.

"Does anyone else live around here besides Estevan?" he asked. He pulled the edge of the curtain back and looked out into the dark yard.

"There's another family a mile up the road, but they wouldn't be here at this time of night." Patrick could see fear in Sonrisa's eyes. "Is there someone out there?"

Patrick didn't want to alarm her, but he also didn't want to be dishonest. "I thought I heard someone, then it was quiet. So, it could have been an animal, but just to be safe, I'll stay up for a while and make sure."

"I thought you had to leave early in the morning?"

"I'll be fine. Get some sleep."

Sonrisa started to answer him, then instead headed to her room.

Patrick listened while Sonrisa settled down. Then the house became quiet. He got out the revolver that Estevan had trained him with, then checked the windows and doors again and sat down to wait. One thing was for certain. If there was someone out there who meant to do harm, Estevan had prepared Patrick to hit a bull's-eye dead center every time. If they had somehow found him and were coming for him, he would do everything in his power to ensure that Sonrisa and Juan didn't get caught in the crossfire.

7

It was in the early morning hours that Patrick heard Juan yelling. He wondered if the boy was having a bad dream, but then he cried, "Let go of me!" Patrick bolted from the couch and ran to Juan's room to see his pajamaed legs disappearing out the window. He raced to the front of the house and flew out the door, but a truck was already speeding out of the driveway. Lightning crossed the sky then, and raindrops began splattering the earth.

Dressed in a long, white nightgown, her hair streaming down her back, Sonrisa ran up next to him, screaming Juan's name.

"Where's your car?" asked Patrick.

"I don't have one. Estevan has the only one, and they're gone. Oh, my God, he has Juan!"

"Who has Juan?"

"Toran, his father. It's got to be him. I didn't think he'd ever find us out here. What am I going to do?" Her eyes looked around wildly, rain wetting her hair and gown. "I'm sorry to have gotten you involved in this," she said as tears began to spill.

"No need to apologize," Patrick said. "Let's go back inside where it's dry." He ran a hand through his tangle of hair, shaking off the raindrops. "I need you to tell me everything."

Once sitting on the couch, Sonrisa clasped her hands together. "Toran is my ex-boyfriend. He wasn't, isn't, a good man. He—she stopped and wiped the tears off her cheeks—hurt me. He never hurt Juan, but I started worrying that he might. I was afraid to leave him, though. He comes from a powerful family. My only recourse was to escape and disappear."

"What does he do?"

"His business is shipping, but his family has organized crime ties. He's from Scotland." Sonrisa looked out the open front door as the smell of wet earth filled the room and thunder rumbled in the distance. "I know you have your own problems, Patrick. You said you have to leave this morning. I don't want my problems to keep you from your own need to be safe."

Patrick checked the time. It would soon be sunrise, and his ride was scheduled to pick him up at seven. "From what you're telling me, it doesn't sound like Toran wants to hurt Juan. He wouldn't have come all this way to get him if that was his intention."

"Maybe not, but God knows what he'll expose him to, and Toran has enemies."

"How does Estevan fit in?" asked Patrick.

"When Toran and I were out one night in Scotland, I happened to run into this woman in a pub. We were in the bathroom washing up, and she noticed my throat." Sonrisa's lower lip trembled, and she glanced down at her hands.

A flush of anger boiled in Patrick's chest. "Bruises?"

Sonrisa didn't look at Patrick, but instead just nodded.

He waited for her to continue.

"She told me there was help. An underground railroad

that got women to safety. That's how I ended up here five thousand miles away. This property belongs to Estevan, and he has let me stay here. Juan was one year old when I left, so this is really the only home he's ever known. It's been so quiet over the last ten years that I thought we were safe. But Toran must have been searching for us this entire time."

"In my experience, men like Toran have very long memories," said Patrick. "Hurry and get dressed. Pack yourself a small bag."

Sonrisa looked up at Patrick. "Pack a bag?"

"Yes, I have a ride coming soon. You need to come with me. We'll figure out what to do on the way. Do you have a cellphone?"

Sonrisa nodded.

"Does Juan have the number?"

"Yes, I had him memorize it in case something happened."

"Does he know about his father?"

Sonrisa hesitated.

"You didn't tell him, did you?"

"No. I didn't want him to know who his father really was, so I told him he was a hero and had died." She swallowed. "I probably should have told him the truth, but the more I could make that time in our life a distant memory, the better. And I didn't think it would serve any purpose for Juan to hate his father. I've found that hate doesn't solve anything. It only causes problems."

Sonrisa stood on unsteady feet and went to her bedroom. She pulled open the closet door and reached on the top shelf for her suitcase, then smacked off the dust and began piling in clothing and toiletries. She dressed quickly in dark pants and a gray blouse, braiding her hair in a long pigtail, then took her phone out of the beside bureau and checked for messages. Nothing. She reassured herself. Patrick was right. Toran wouldn't have come all this way to hurt Juan. He wanted her son for himself.

In the kitchen, she found Patrick slugging down coffee. "There's more, if you want," he said.

Sonrisa picked up a mug from the counter that she had made with Juan on her pottery wheel. She held back tears as she filled it, then took a drink, hands shaking.

Patrick went to the front door and stood there watching the road that led to the house. The thunderstorm had finished, and now hazy early morning light filtered into the house on the humid air. He turned to her and asked, "You have everything you need?"

Sonrisa gasped. "Juan's asthma medicine. He needs to take it every day."

She turned toward her son's room as Patrick said, "We'll find him."

"Thank you," she said, the words coming out choked. Then she went to grab the bottle of pills from his bedside table. When she returned to the living room, she could see a car in the distance. She stood beside Patrick, her suitcase in hand. She hadn't known him long, but she trusted Patrick. And at this point, he was the only hope she had of ever seeing her son again.

8

The SUV pulled up and Patrick noted the driver was not the same person who had dropped him off. This man, slightly hunched, wire glasses perched on his nose, looked at them with questions in his eyes. "I was told I was picking up one person."

Patrick kept his tone matter-of-fact. "She needs a ride out." Then he stared down the driver, who finally motioned with his shoulder for them to get in.

Patrick opened the back door and waited for Sonrisa to climb in, then did the same.

Without saying another word, the driver stepped on the gas and headed away from Sonrisa's house. She glanced back only once, then turned to stare straight ahead. She and Patrick sat close, and he could feel her trembling. He had the urge to comfort her, so he took her hand in his. A surprised expression crossed her face. Patrick just continued to hold her hand as he focused on the landscape outside the window.

Sonrisa knew Patrick was likely holding her hand because he felt badly for her. Nevertheless, it gave her a feeling of support and comfort. "Thank you for getting me away from the house. I would have lost my mind if I'd been stuck there," she said.

"Every problem has a solution," said Patrick.

Sonrisa nodded as her thoughts turned to Juan, so alone and afraid without her. He didn't remember his father; he had only been a baby when they left. Toran obviously hadn't stopped looking for his son, even after a decade. She shuddered to think how angry he must be—how his outrage had likely deepened with each passing year. Juan was a sweet boy, still tender, but with a belief in himself and a natural ability to judge situations. She prayed he would be okay.

They pulled in front of a hotel a couple of hours later. The driver waited until Patrick and Sonrisa got out and retrieved their luggage, then drove away without a backward glance. Sonrisa looked at Patrick, half expecting him to announce their plans, but he just pointed to the lobby with a lift of his chin, then took her bag and headed that way. At the front desk, a man greeted them. "*Hola y bienvenidos a Hotel de Tabasco.*"

"*Gracias,*" said Patrick. "*Soy* Ronald Tempor."

The man's eyes lit up in recognition at the name. He looked around the lobby, then reached underneath the desk and pulled out a manila envelope, handing it to Patrick. Then he glanced at Sonrisa. "Do you need two rooms?"

"One room with two beds will be fine," said Patrick. The last thing he wanted was for Sonrisa to be alone, too terror-stricken to sleep.

When they were by themselves in the elevator heading up to the fifth floor, Sonrisa asked, "Your name isn't Patrick?"

Patrick knitted his brows together. "Patrick is my name. Tempor is an alias. Things aren't always as they appear."

Lips pressed together, she searched his eyes, then said quietly, "Yes, that's what I've learned in life."

When they got into the room, Patrick took a deep breath. With the new development of Juan's kidnapping, and the unknown influence of this Toran character, he worried about Sonrisa's safety. He needed to tell her what he was doing here in Mexico. The last thing he wanted was for her to doubt him. She already looked uncomfortable.

He walked over to the hotel mini-fridge and took out an inexpensive bottle of white wine. Then he found two glasses in the bathroom and half-filled them. He set the wine on a small table and pulled out a chair. Then he gestured to Sonrisa to join him. She followed, and they sat facing each other.

Patrick steepled his hands in front of him on the table, considering his words. "I know I insisted on you coming with me, and I feel like I owe you an explanation as to why I'm using an alias, and what I'm involved in."

Sonrisa didn't say anything as Patrick took a sip of wine, then leaned back in his chair. "I'm on what seems to have become a never-ending mission. It's for some powerful people in Central America. The background on how I got into this situation is long and convoluted, but the bottom line is that I have been hiding in Mexico for the last several years to protect myself and my family back home in New Jersey. Now is my opportunity to complete the mission so that I can resume my life in the States, if that's even possible." He paused. "With that said, I know your thoughts are probably consumed with Juan right now. Tell me more about Toran, so we can strategize on getting Juan back safely."

Sonrisa swirled the wine in the glass, then took a deep breath and began. "Toran's last name is Murray, and his family..." She didn't finish her sentence but stopped to push her hair behind one ear. Patrick could see anxiety mapped across her face. "I'm originally from the Bay area," she continued. "I was in an art exchange program in France when Toran and I met twelve years ago. He was there on business." She looked down at the table. "I was young and naïve at the time, and he was so charming and dashing. When I look back, I realize there were signs from the beginning that I ignored. It wasn't long before he began telling me what I could do, and what I'd better not do without his permission. I told myself he bossed me around because he loved me so much and wanted me to be safe. But now I know it was all about control. Whenever I did what I thought was best for me and went against his wishes, he began enforcing his rules in his way, and he became harsher and crueler as time went on."

She swallowed and Patrick waited for her to resume.

"At first, he thought my art was interesting, and he encouraged me. He asked everything about my life, like where I grew up and what I thought about my art teacher. Did I find him attractive? Did I go out with the other students? What did I do with my spare time? I was happy he was so interested in my life. At our student art show, he impressed my fellow students and the instructors by buying all my pieces. Can you imagine? I had never experienced anyone who seemed so generous and thoughtful. When it was time for me to return home to the Bay area and art school, he begged me to stay with him in Europe. He rented an apartment in France and told me I could paint there while he did business, and we'd travel back and forth to the family estate in Scotland. It seemed like a fairy tale, and I was the princess. Like I said, I was young, naïve, and stupid." She looked over at Patrick, eyes moist.

"Young, naïve, and stupid is what got me here," said Patrick. "I understand."

Sonrisa gave him a half smile.

Patrick sat forward. "How did Juan come into the picture?"

"When Toran moved me into his apartment in France, he became increasingly demanding of my time, and when he drank too much, he was cruel." Her eyes revealed her pain. "Though I set up an art studio in the apartment, I rarely had the opportunity to paint. It was a rollercoaster existence with him. One day he would hurt me, and the next apologize with gifts. I discovered from the people who helped me get away from him that this is the typical cycle of abuse. It turns out that my situation was a textbook case." She shook her head, then took a sip of wine. "In a weird way that made me feel better to know I wasn't the only one."

She sighed, then continued, "Once I figured out that life with Toran was always going to be chaotic and painful, I began working on a way to leave. I had gotten a ticket home, but he found out and became enraged. He destroyed the ticket and assigned me a bodyguard, saying that it was for my own safety, but I knew the man was meant to keep tabs on me and ensure I didn't try to leave. Not long after that, I discovered I was pregnant, even though we had been using protection. At that point, he insisted we go to the family estate in Scotland so I could have the baby there."

"I'm sure the pregnancy was calculated on his part," Patrick said. "The subject of marriage didn't come up?"

"Toran brought it up a few times, but always dropped it. I suspect he didn't want me to have access to the family funds. By then I'd seen the real him and didn't want to marry him anyway." A tear slid down Sonrisa's cheek, and she brushed it away. "One thing I can say for sure, though Juan wasn't conceived in love, he means the world to me. Though I had to endure Toran's wrath, I haven't for one moment regretted having Juan. And if I have to endure Toran's wrath to get Juan back and ensure his safety, I won't hesitate."

9

Moved by the tenderness and resolution in her voice when she spoke of Juan, Patrick said, "You may have been naïve when you met Toran, but you've been an excellent mother to Juan. He knows you love him, and he has a good head on his shoulders. I'm sure he's okay."

Sonrisa nodded her head vigorously, then gave him a watery smile. "Thanks for reminding me of that."

"The people who helped you get free from Toran," said Patrick, "do you know where they are based?"

"Someone met me and Juan at the edge of Toran's property in the middle of the night. There were several stops along the way before we made it to Estevan's, but I couldn't tell where we were."

"Is your real name Sonrisa?"

Sonrisa's eyes flashed at Patrick, then she looked away and bit her lip. After a moment, she turned back. "My given name is Andrea Black. Estevan encouraged me to choose a new name. I knew that *sonrisa* meant smile in Spanish, so I decided that I wanted to be reminded of how lucky I was to have escaped Toran. I became Sonrisa Herrera."

"Did the name help?"

Sonrisa smiled. "It did. I also renamed Juan. His birth name is Callum."

"I think I have someone I can call for help with Juan," he said. "Give me a minute. Do you want something to eat? We could order room service. I'll take a burger."

Sonrisa picked up a menu while Patrick opened the envelope the desk clerk had given him. The message was on parchment paper and had been written by what looked like a quill pen. *"Go to the ruins of Moral Reforma in Tabasco tonight at midnight under the full moon. You will see an entry point in the northwest corner of the tomb. You will know what to do once there. You have twelve hours to complete this retrieval or forfeit."* It was accompanied by a map of the ruins and surrounding area.

Patrick slid the instructions back into the envelope, then strummed his fingers on the table as he glanced at his phone. He hated to make the phone call and put anyone at risk, but he didn't know who else to reach out to for help with Juan. He pushed the number and waited.

"Agent Tomlinson."

"It's me."

"Patrick? Is everything okay?" asked his sister.

"I'm okay. I'm working on that plan I told you about to get home. This line is secure?"

"Yes. Do you need help?"

Patrick looked over at Sonrisa, who had hung up the phone after ordering a meal. "Not for me. For someone else."

"Oh, who?"

"A woman I met in Veracruz. I was staying at her place during my extraction. Her son was kidnapped this morning by his father."

"Patrick, that is a case for the local authorities."

"It's a sensitive issue. The father, Toran Murray, has Scottish organized crime ties and is very dangerous. I'm just trying to help her get her son back."

"While also trying to save yourself."

Patrick sighed. "Can you offer me any direction?"

"Let me talk to Savannah, my boss. She has connections with Interpol."

"I really appreciate it."

His sister was silent for a moment. "So, you're getting closer to coming home?" Patrick could hear the hope in her voice.

"If all goes well, I should be seeing you soon."

"That would make my year," said Cherie.

Patrick stood in the alleyway near the gas station, his breath coming in quick gasps. He had done what Frankie ordered—taken photos of all the key areas—but the owner had caught him and run Patrick off, yelling to not come back or he'd call the cops. Patrick added in his head how much more money he needed for his mother's car repair. Then he could get out of this mess.

Anxiety rippled through him when he thought about the conversation he'd overheard amongst Frankie's men. One of the guys had wanted out, and from what Patrick could tell, it didn't go too well. He'd been beaten so badly that now he couldn't walk. Leaning against the grimy alley wall, Patrick focused on steadying his breathing. He'd find a way out. He had to.

A half hour later, Patrick stood in Frankie's apartment watching his face turn an alarming red-colored shade.

"How hard could it have been to take a few photos without getting caught?" he yelled at Patrick.

"Sorry."

Frankie backhanded him across the face. "Don't ever say you're sorry. You hear me? That's a sign of weakness. None of my crew is weak. Stupid sometimes, but never weak."

Patrick kept his face immobile, willing himself not to move. His jaw felt sore, but he didn't touch it.

Frankie hit his fist into his palm a couple of times, and Patrick braced to get hit again. But instead, Frankie said, "You can make good money with me, kid, but you gotta buck up. Can you do that?"

Patrick nodded.

"Go back to the gas station and figure out if they have a silent alarm. Find out where it's located. And how long it would take to get to the safe in the back room. Go back when the owner isn't there. You get that done, I've got a big payday for you."

Cherie called back just as Patrick was finishing his hamburger. He wiped his mouth and answered.

"I have an Interpol contact for you," she said. "An American working out of the national headquarters in France. He's tapped into Northern European organized crime and can maybe help. Name is Lance Gray."

When Patrick hung up the phone, Sonrisa, who had only picked at her food, looked at him expectantly.

"There may be someone who can help us. I'm going to put our conversation on speaker phone."

Sonrisa nodded. "Okay, thank you."

Patrick punched in the number Cherie had given him. A voice said, "Who's calling?"

"My name is Patrick Tomlinson, Mr. Gray."

"Oh, yes, Savannah Sanchez told me you'd be calling. You can call me Lance. I understand there is a missing boy?"

Patrick explained the situation.

When he'd finished, the man replied, "I can check into this, but we're going to have a big problem. From what you've told me, the mother essentially kidnapped the boy when he was one year old. If you want to get technical about this, and believe me, the Scottish Embassy and authorities there will, the boy's father was simply taking back his son. The manner in which the boy was taken this morning is alarming, but the lawyers will say that it was no different than her leaving with him ten years ago."

This was something Patrick hadn't considered. "Well, the boy went against his free will."

"That could work in your favor. And you say Murray was beating the mother? Does she have proof of the injuries? Any visits to hospitals? Photos?"

Patrick looked at Sonrisa. "I have the mother with me right now."

"I visited the hospital in Scotland several times," said Sonrisa. "Once when he broke my clavicle."

"Okay, let me make some calls and get back to you. I've got a source in Scotland who can check things out. I'll see if we can get eyes on your boy."

"That would be such a relief," said Sonrisa. "Thank you."

When Patrick hung up, Sonrisa said, "I don't know how I can thank you."

"Family is important," said Patrick, feeling the pangs of his own separation. "I take it you left family back in the Bay area?"

Sonrisa's expression saddened. "My mother and father, and sister, Teresa."

"They don't know where you are?"

Sonrisa shook her head. "I was able to get word to them through Estevan, but they only know I'm safe. I haven't seen them since I left the States twelve years ago."

Patrick thought about how his own family who, except for Cherie just recently, thought he was dead. He wished he could have gotten word to them when he left Jersey, but that would have gotten them killed, and until he finished this mission, they were still in danger.

When there was still no word from the Interpol contact by late afternoon, Patrick began to prepare for his trek to Moral Reforma. While he didn't need to be there until midnight, he wanted to head out early, should the drive take longer than expected. But more importantly, to learn the area, in case there were any surprises.

"You're going somewhere?" asked Sonrisa, anxiety in her tone. She scooted to the edge of her seat.

Only for a few hours. "I have to pick up some information tonight."

"Can I come with you?" she asked. "It'll keep my mind off Juan."

Patrick thought for a moment. "It's a two-hour drive," he said.

"Whether I'm waiting in the car or waiting here, I'm still waiting," she said. "Besides, I'll be on hand if the Interpol agent calls you."

"This isn't the place for you, Sonrisa. It might be dangerous. I'm not sure what I'm getting myself into."

"I'm going," she said, standing up.

Patrick could tell her mind was made up.

They found a taxi in front of the hotel. When Patrick leaned his head in the passenger side, the driver, a middle-aged man with a scruffy beard, quickly wrapped up the burrito he was eating and exclaimed, "You need a ride?"

"We'd like to go to Moral Reforma."

"Tomorrow? It closes soon."

"No, tonight."

The man's eyebrows raised.

"I'll pay double what you usually charge," said Patrick.

The man tapped his chest. "Enrique will take you!"

Patrick opened the back door and waited for Sonrisa to slide in, then got in after her.

The driver peered at them in the rearview mirror and said, "*Dos horas*, and the second half of the trip the roads have no concrete, very rough."

Sonrisa tried to relax as they made their way to the pyramid, but she kept thinking about Juan. Was he at Toran's estate in Scotland, or was Toran hiding him somewhere else? She never thought Juan would see his father again, and now she wondered if it had been such a good idea to keep the truth from him. In addition to being scared and confused, he was probably angry with her for not telling him.

It was warm in the car, and it smelled of tortilla and beans. After a while, Sonrisa found her eyes getting heavy. She laid her head back on the seat.

Patrick looked over at Sonrisa to see her eyes closed. After a bit, her face became more relaxed, and she looked almost peaceful. Visions of her safely in her studio, humming, hands smeared with paint, tugged at him. He thought about his own situation being on the run, then imagined having a child in tow. The stress on her must be tremendous. He admired how she had kept it together. From his short time with Juan, he could see that Sonrisa had given him a good upbringing. He was a happy boy, funny, affectionate with his mother, always content to be around her. Patrick couldn't help thinking of his own mother then, and the pain he had caused her over the last several years. He wondered how she would react when he returned home. Would she be angry, relieved, or not believe her eyes?

An hour later, the sun had set and the sky was dark, except for the moon, when the driver swung onto an unpaved road. "Sorry, *Señor y Señorita*," he announced as the car began bumping in and out of potholes.

Sonrisa stirred, opening her eyes and focusing on Patrick's face in the dim light. "He wasn't kidding about the rough road." She yawned.

Patrick pulled out the map and shined his flashlight on it.

"We have very good weather here, lots of heat and sunshine, but then it rains." The taxi driver laughed. "The roads become full of holes." He went back to concentrating on driving.

Sonrisa leaned closer to Patrick, eyeing the page. "That's where we're going? May I see?"

He handed the paper to her, and she studied it. "I've heard of this area. About ten years ago, they started excavating the pyramids there. I thought about taking Juan awhile back, but I was always so concerned about being seen."

"How do you think Toran found you?" asked Patrick.

Sonrisa was quiet for a minute. "Most likely from my art. Over the years, I've told Francisco, the owner of the art gallery where my paintings are shown, that I prefer to stay out of the public eye as much as possible, in terms of photos of myself. I think he thought I was just shy. There was a showing last month of my work, and they took photos that appeared in the local paper. I'd hoped it would slip under the radar, but I was apparently wrong. Now that I look back, maybe I should have taken Juan and left then. By wanting to continue my art, perhaps I jeopardized us." A look of remorse crossed her face.

"Powerful men tend to have eyes all over the globe," commented Patrick, almost to himself.

"There ain't no point in trying to outrun the boss. He always finds people," said Nick, Frankie's right-hand man and cousin, a short bruiser who wore a baseball cap tipped on the back of his head and bright white tennis shoes. "If he thinks you let him down, he'll find you, and then no one will ever find you, if you get my drift."

The two were sitting in Frankie's apartment one night

waiting for their orders. Patrick sensed Nick was giving him a warning to not run out on the night's plan.

"Frankie's in an even worse mood than usual," said Nick. "Suzette moved out."

Patrick thought about how he hadn't seen her in a few days. He wasn't about to ask what happened.

Just then the front door banged open and Frankie entered, scowling.

Nick jumped up and Patrick followed. Frankie barked at one of the men who accompanied him, "Stand outside and do your frigging job." He pointed to another of the men. "Pour me a stiff one."

Then he turned to Patrick and Nick. "You two ready for tonight? You damn well better be. I need this haul." He pointed to Nick. "You explained what he's going to do, right?"

"Yeah, Frankie. We been over it a dozen times."

"Well, go over it a dozen more. Then get out of here and get it done. And wear the ski masks."

11

When they arrived at the pyramid, the massive hulk of the structure appeared formless in the dark night. Enrique parked and pointed. "That is Moral Reforma."

"We won't be long, but we're counting on you to take us back," said Patrick. "You can expect something extra for your trouble."

"I am here," said Enrique, turning off the engine.

They got out of the car and set off toward the pyramid, Patrick shining the flashlight on the ground so they could both see the way.

"What are we looking for?" asked Sonrisa.

"Clues as to the location of an antiquity. The note said to look for an inset on the north wall."

"So, we're on a treasure hunt of sorts?"

Patrick stopped walking and shined the flashlight ahead of them. He turned then to look at her. "Yes, and the stakes are high." He spotted an area on the pyramid that appeared to be recessed and pointed that way with the flashlight.

"Why did you need training from Estevan to collect clues?" asked Sonrisa.

Patrick glanced over at her.

"I'm sorry, I'm probably talking too much and asking too many questions," she said.

"I was just thinking this is the most I've heard you talk since we met." Patrick smiled at her in the darkness. They were only a few feet from the pyramid. He stopped to illuminate the stone's rough surface when Sonrisa pointed and said, "I see something in between those two layers there."

Patrick directed the light to the crevice. There was what looked like paper wedged in there. He gave the flashlight to Sonrisa, then walked over and knelt in front of the side of the pyramid. Reaching into the crevice, he secured the paper between his forefinger and thumb and pulled it out. He peered at it in the moonlight. More instructions. He folded the paper and slid it into his pocket.

They were heading back to the car when Patrick heard someone moving across the gravel behind them. "Run to the car," he shouted at her. "If something happens, have Enrique just drive away."

"But—" Sonrisa said, alarmed.

"Just go!"

Sonrisa turned to run, and Patrick swung around just as a man jumped at him. They ended up tussling on the ground until Patrick was able to get him in a vice grip. But then the man's arm flew up and lobbed the side of Patrick's skull with what must have been a rock. A jolt of pain traveled throughout his head and neck, and he fell to the ground.

"Give it to me," the man ordered as he kneeled over Patrick.

Feigning unconsciousness, Patrick remained still. When the man motioned to search Patrick's pocket, he sprang to life and shoved him backward. His assailant went flying to the ground just as car lights advanced toward them. Sonrisa leaned out of the window and cried, "Get in!"

Patrick leapt up and ran to hop into the back seat as a terrified Enrique turned the car around and sped over the unpaved road, the car bouncing up and down as they headed away from the pyramid.

"*Dios mío!*" Enrique cried.

Patrick felt something wet on the side of his head and then saw that his fingers were bloody.

"You're hurt," exclaimed Sonrisa. She used the flashlight to examine his head. "The skin is broken."

Patrick glanced out the back window.

"We didn't see any other car out here," she said. "What did he want? The paper?"

Patrick nodded, then winced at the pain. "He tried but didn't get it from me."

Sonrisa wasn't sure what she had just stepped into. She took a deep breath and focused on holding her bandana to the gash on Patrick's head. "How are you feeling?" she asked after some time.

"A little dizzy, but I think I'll be okay." He gently took the bandana from her hand. "I can hold it, thank you."

They rode in silence for a time, Enrique glancing back at them, a wary expression in his eyes.

"I'm sorry about what happened," Patrick told him. "I didn't think anyone would be out there."

Enrique nodded but didn't say anything. Instead, he drove the car even faster as they rattled along.

Patrick's cellphone lit up then. He looked at the screen. "It's Lance at Interpol."

Sonrisa held her breath as he answered.

"Lance, yes, this is a good time." Patrick listened intently. "And you're sure?" He glanced at Sonrisa. "Yes, that will help set her mind at rest." Then Patrick's brow furrowed. "Okay, thank you. Please do."

"What did he say?" asked Sonrisa when Patrick hung up.

"That it was Toran who took Juan. Toran has him at the Murray estate in Edinburgh."

"And Juan is okay?"

"As far as Lance's source can tell, yes. In fact, Toran appears to be treating him well."

Sonrisa let out a big breath. "What about getting him back?"

Patrick sighed. "Toran is claiming you kidnapped Juan when he was a baby. The Scottish authorities are now involved. Given that Juan is also a Scottish citizen by birth, things aren't so cut-and-dried."

"Oh, my God, am I ever going to see my baby again?" Sonrisa put her head in her hands.

"Lance is trying to find some options. Since Juan is also a US citizen, Lance might have some luck with the US Embassy. The problem is you've been living under the radar in Mexico these past years." Patrick put his hand on Sonrisa's shoulder. "Just remind yourself that we know where Juan is and that he appears to be well."

Sonrisa nodded. "That's the most important thing."

"What if you tried to talk to Toran about considering a compromise? Would he listen?" asked Patrick.

Sonrisa looked down at her hands, then back up at Patrick.

"Is there something you're not telling me?" asked Patrick.

Just then Enrique announced, "We are almost to the highway."

"Thank you," Patrick said to the man. "You'll be well paid for tonight." He redirected his attention to Sonrisa.

Sonrisa had been careful in her new life to not let the secret she protected get out. She stared straight ahead but could feel Patrick's eyes on her. Finally, she spoke, "I took something when I left."

"What?"

"A necklace that has been handed down through the generations. It dates back to the 1700s. It was kept in a display case in the family estate in Scotland."

12

"Where is the necklace now?" Patrick asked.

"Hidden at my house in Veracruz."

He paused, considering her confession, then checked to see if his head was still bleeding. "Why did you take it?"

"I thought I could use it as a bargaining chip should Toran come after me. It's very important to the family. Toran wouldn't even let me touch it."

"Do you think he knows you took it?"

Surprise flashed through Sonrisa's eyes. "I always assumed he did. I never even considered he might not know."

Patrick felt a dull ache starting to grow in his head now. He laid his head back on the seat and closed his eyes.

Back at the hotel, Patrick gave Enrique a generous payment, then they passed through the lobby and up to their room. Once inside, Sonrisa said, "I think we should clean off the gash on your head, then you need to lie down. I'll get some ice."

Patrick went into the bathroom and leaned against the

counter while Sonrisa got a washcloth wet. "This is probably going to hurt," she said, dabbing at the wound. He remained still as she cleaned it out, rinsing the washcloth several times. They stood inches from one another, and Patrick could feel the pull he'd been experiencing from the moment they'd met. At one point, Sonrisa paused and met his gaze, then her face flushed slightly. She examined the side of his head. "It looks pretty clean now. Fortunately, it's not that deep of a wound. I have some antibiotic ointment that I can put on it."

"Well prepared, I like that," said Patrick.

"Juan is always scraping his knees or elbows. Why don't you go lie down."

Patrick nodded, suddenly feeling fatigue wash through him.

Sonrisa pulled the covers down on Patrick's bed for him, then grabbed the plastic ice pitcher and left the room. She stood out in the hallway for a moment, trying to quell the mix of emotions she felt. Being close to Patrick brought forth sensations she hadn't felt in a long time. Did he feel the same?

She filled the plastic bin at the ice maker and went back to the room and wrapped a handful of ice in a small towel. Then she sat down on the bed next to Patrick. He appeared to be dozing, then opened his eyes.

"How are you doing? she asked.

"It's hurting a bit more, but I'll be fine," he said. He took hold of her hand, seemingly without realizing it. Sonrisa loved the way his fingers wrapped around hers, and the comfort she felt being this close to him.

"Let me put ice on the side of your head for a while to reduce the inflammation," she said. "I'm going to monitor you tonight, in case you have a concussion."

Patrick smiled. "I think that's an old wives' tale."

"It's an old wives' tale that you shouldn't sleep. Not that you shouldn't be monitored," said Sonrisa.

"Okay, doctor, monitor me. And while you're at it, tell me about what the passion for art is like."

Sonrisa felt a fluttering in her heart at his words. That he was interested, thrilled her. "Where should I start?"

"How about the first time you remember doing a piece of art. How old were you?"

The memory made Sonrisa feel happy. "I was eight. I drew a picture of my grandmother during art time at school. The teacher asked me where I learned to draw so well."

"Where did you learn to draw?"

"Nowhere. I just understood things about art, I guess. Looking back on the drawing now, it was pretty rudimentary, but I think the teacher saw my overall talent. Later, when I was in high school, I began taking art lessons during summer breaks. I'd save the tuition money during the school year babysitting. By then, I was painting every free moment I had, sometimes far into the night. Art fires me up and excites me in a way that nothing else does. In some ways, it's an obsession, but an exciting one."

Sonrisa removed the towel from Patrick's head. "It looks less swollen, but the broken skin looks pretty red. I'm going to dry it and put on the ointment. I might also have some children's pain reliever. You could triple up on the medicine."

Patrick laughed. "I'll take it." He touched his head lightly, and grimaced.

Sonrisa got up to dig through her bag, then handed

Patrick the bottle. "You might as well down what's left." Once he'd done so, she applied some medicine onto his wound. "What about you? What was it like growing up in New Jersey?"

Patrick's face became clouded.

"I'm sorry—" started Sonrisa.

"It's okay. There was a lot that was good. Especially before my dad died."

"Oh, I hadn't realized."

"He was in the Army and died in combat in Afghanistan."

Sonrisa sat back down on the bed. "How old were you?"

"Ten."

Younger than Juan, thought Sonrisa. "That must have been tough."

"It was. My mom was a nurse and did her best but it was hard to make ends meet. We had my father's money from the military, but with three kids…" Patrick was quiet for a moment, then he said suddenly, "When I was in high school, I took on risky jobs to help pay the bills."

"Oh," said Sonrisa. "What kind of jobs?"

Patrick shifted in the bed and winced. "Not anything I'm proud of." He closed his eyes.

Sonrisa waited for him to continue. When he didn't, she shut off the bedside lamp and was about to get up when he put his hand gently on her arm. "Thank you for sharing with me," he murmured. "I'm sorry I'm not better company."

Nick pulled a revolver out of his back pocket.

Patrick looked at the weapon, alarmed. This was the first time they had brought a gun along for a job.

"You know what to do. Scare him so he empties the safe. You both got me?" He looked from Nick to Patrick.

Patrick nodded.

"I can't hear you," said Frankie.

"Got it, Frankie," said Patrick.

"Yeah, got it," said Nick.

Frankie nodded. "You pull this off, we'll be taking back the southwest territory. Nobody is gonna stop Frankie now."

13

Sonrisa watched Patrick as he dozed, wishing he was still awake so they could talk some more. She wanted to learn more about this man. It had been a very long time since she'd felt interested in anyone, and she couldn't help but be attracted to him. He had such a good heart. And she trusted him. Her emotions were already betraying her.

She decided to take a quick shower. Grabbing her suitcase, she went into the bathroom and softly closed the door. She thought about Juan again, feeling a tug of worry in her heart. Then she reminded herself what the Interpol agent had said. Juan was okay. Toran was likely plying their son with video games and whatever he wanted straight from the cook's kitchen. She recalled the honeymoon phase with Toran. How he had done the same with her.

After showering, Sonrisa went back out to find Patrick still asleep. She tiptoed over to him and watched his chest rise and fall for a moment, then slipped into the other bed and pulled up the covers. For a while she stayed awake, monitoring his breathing, which remained steady, but after some time her eyelids began to feel heavy.

. . .

It was morning when Sonrisa awoke to streams of light filtering across the bedspread from under the curtains. For a moment, she was disoriented, then she remembered where she was. Patrick wasn't lying in his bed anymore. She heard the shower going. Some nurse she turned out to be, sleeping through the night. She thought of Juan. Was he wondering why she hadn't rescued him yet? Just then, Patrick came out of the bathroom dressed in jeans. Sonrisa looked at his chest, moist from the shower, then away.

"You're awake," he said, giving her a quick smile. "I survived the night."

Sonrisa sat up in bed. "It wasn't my nursing skills that helped you survive. How is your head?"

"There's a pretty bad bruise, but the wound is minor. I'll be okay."

Patrick was having a hard time focusing with Sonrisa in her nightgown. Though it was a simple blue gown that wasn't at all revealing, he couldn't help but imagine underneath, and that made his insides heat up.

"Want me to put more ointment on your wound?" she asked.

"If you wouldn't mind."

Sonrisa got out of the bed and went to her bag. She brought the ointment to him and parted his hair. "It's still swollen, but you're right, the wound looks pretty superficial."

She squeezed out some ointment, then began to dab it on with her fingertip. "A couple more times of this, and it'll probably be healed."

When she finished, Patrick said, "Thank you for that."

They remained motionless for a time, looking into each other's eyes. Sonrisa was about to turn away when Patrick gently pulled her to him and placed his lips on hers. He could feel her hesitation, so he stopped. "I'm sorry, I probably shouldn't have done that. I didn't mean to take advantage of the situation."

"No need to apologize," she said. "It's just been so long."

Patrick nodded and was about to tell her it was the same for him, but there was a noise at the door. A piece of paper slipped beneath it onto the floor. He went over and opened it.

Your next stop is Comalcalco. Consult the information from last night for details. Do not tarry. You must arrive at the site by midnight. Take caution to avoid attack from the enemy.

Patrick set the message on the table, then pulled the paper from the night before from his pocket and unfolded it. He placed that message next to the other and read it. *From the corner of the stage to the northwest quadrant, walk forty paces, then turn around to face the moon and walk forty more. On the fortieth step you will be facing the hiding place. Locate the information you seek.*

He looked from one note to the other and shook his head. Was someone just pulling his chain with all of this?

"You have a not-so-good look on your face," said Sonrisa. "I'm pretty good at problem solving."

"I don't know if any of this will make sense," he said. "It doesn't make sense to me."

"Try me."

"About three years ago, someone sent me a letter here in

Mexico, claiming to know my predicament and offering me a way out. At first, I was alarmed. I'd been careful about staying hidden to keep my family safe. I was considering leaving my home in Puerto Vallarta to find another place to hide when I got a call." Patrick paused, thinking how this sounded even crazier when he said it out loud.

Sonrisa came over to pull out a chair at the table and sat down.

"I'm not sure how he found me. It could have been he was monitoring my activity at the Puerto Vallarta Library. For the last several years, just for fun, I've been researching the lost Maya artifacts. The man who called said he would help me if I helped him."

Sonrisa nodded. "Sounds like an even trade, unless he wanted you to do something terrible."

"He presented it more like a series of high-risk treasure hunts. I was always good at problem solving, and I'd been reading about the Maya ruins for years. I agreed to give it a try and began pointing out spots where yet to be located treasures might be hiding. He paid me for my services, which helped me stay afloat. But more importantly, he kept talking about how they were preparing me to go home."

"Who is they?"

Patrick looked at the notes on the table. "From what I can tell, my contact represents a group of wealthy individuals interested in protecting antiquities. They are a part of what is known as The Cause, *La Causa*, the same organization that Estevan once worked for."

"How could they help you get home?"

"I don't know. Of course, their saying that got my attention. But in all honesty, I figured that mentioning me going home was just their way to get me interested. A couple of months ago, though, I got a message telling me that after one last mission, I would be returning to the States. Then I received a newspaper clipping from home."

Sonrisa was leaning forward by now, appearing to hang on his every word.

Patrick swallowed. He wasn't sure if he should tell her the contents of the article. Then his phone began ringing.

14

"It could be about Juan," said Patrick, springing up to grab his phone from the bedside table.

"I've got some good news," said Lance when he answered. "Murray has agreed to let the boy speak to his mother briefly tomorrow morning at six am his time."

"That is good news," said Patrick. "What's the temperature with him?"

"It's a diplomatic mess. I'm working to liaison between the American and Scottish Embassies. It's a case of he said, she said. The fact that the mother kidnapped the boy and kept him away from the father for a decade is not working in her favor. On the other side of the coin, she didn't pull the boy out of bed in the middle of the night and spirit him off like Murray just did. You'll likely be hearing from Heidi Monroe with the US Embassy. As for the phone call, the boy has been very upset about being taken from his mother; hence Murray allowing the communication."

"How will it happen??"

"Sonrisa is to call a secure line. Murray said it was for

security's sake, but we both know it's so you can't track the boy's whereabouts."

"Has he moved him from the family estate?"

"Possibly. To protect Sonrisa's location, I would tell her to get a burner phone. I'll text the number she is to call."

Patrick hung up and looked over at Sonrisa, whose expression was anxious.

"Lance has arranged for you to speak to Juan for a few minutes tonight at midnight our time."

"Really? Oh, Patrick, that's wonderful news," said Sonrisa. Tears sprang to her eyes, and she reached for a tissue. "Thank you so much for helping to arrange that."

"Someone with the US Embassy is taking over. We also need to get you a burner phone to protect your whereabouts."

Sonrisa nodded, her expression serious.

Patrick checked the time. Only eleven am. Comalcalco was a four-hour drive. If he left by midafternoon, he would arrive in plenty of time for tonight's deadline. Given what happened last night, he would rent a car for the excursion so he wouldn't be putting another innocent driver in harm's way.

"I have to go out later to the next location for the mission," he told her. "I wouldn't advise going with me, because it may be dangerous, and I don't know if we'll have reception. You don't want to miss making the call."

Sonrisa would have liked it if Patrick was by her side when she talked to Toran. But she said, "I understand."

A few minutes later, after she dressed in a tie-dyed skirt and matching blue top, they headed into town to get a burner phone and have lunch. They found a little restaurant, where they ordered a plate of enchiladas and flan for dessert. As they waited for their lunch, a mariachi band made their way toward Sonrisa and Patrick. The leader gave them a bow, then signaled for his band to play. As his backup musicians strummed their *guitarrones* with gusto, he belted out a tune about love lost and found. When he finished and they gave them a standing ovation, Patrick handed the man some pesos.

"That was fun," said Sonrisa when the band left their table and started playing across the restaurant. As she said that, she realized she hadn't worried about Juan for a whole five minutes.

The waitress came with their food then and asked, "*Algo más?*"

"*No, gracias*, nothing more," answered Sonrisa.

They both dug in, neither speaking for a while. When her plate was empty of enchiladas, Sonrisa slid a spoon through the silken flan. "I'm so full, but I never pass up dessert."

Patrick smiled. "You have a sweet tooth?"

Sonrisa laughed. "That's an understatement. I always have Juan hide the cookies after we make them, or else I can't stop myself." The words made a lump form in her throat. Her heart ached with longing to wrap her arms around her son.

Patrick took a big spoonful of the flan. "I have a sweet tooth, too."

"A man with a sweet tooth, I like that," said Sonrisa, anxious to change the subject. "Most of the men I've known have had a weak spot for alcohol." She frowned. "I'm sorry. I shouldn't be making comparisons."

Patrick took another spoonful. "Comparisons can show you how far you've come."

It wasn't so bad working for Frankie, Patrick told himself. Though the jobs were unsettling, he was now able to give his mother money on a regular basis. She had fixed things in the house and was paid up on the mortgage. He was often tired at school, but coffee and sugar kept him going. And he wasn't going to do this forever. College was coming up next year.

As he started to head up to Frankie's apartment one night, he heard shouting. He stopped at the foot of the stairs. It sounded like Frankie was standing right outside of his front door.

"You tell Sal that if he steps foot in my territory again, I'll break his head open." Silence for a moment, then Frankie spoke again. "Yeah, well, I've got my own army, and it's growing every day. Let him know that." Quiet again, then Frankie exploded. "I've got an operation brewing that's going to put me at the top of the heap."

"What the hell are you doing?" said a voice behind him. Patrick jumped and turned around to see Nick coming toward him.

"The boss was on the phone, so I was waiting until he finished. He was doing a lot of yelling."

Nick pushed past Patrick. "He's always yelling. Be glad he's not yelling at you."

Patrick followed Nick up to Frankie's apartment to find the boss inside pouring himself a tall glass of beer. "There you are," he said, taking a few slugs, then slamming it down. "Last week was a dress rehearsal. Tonight—the real deal." He turned to Nick. "You got it?"

15

Before Patrick headed out that night, he assured Sonrisa, "I'll be back before you know it. Just keep the door locked. I wish I could be here when you talk to Juan."

Sonrisa hugged her arms around her body, her anxiety threatening to take over. "You've done more than enough for me already. I'll be fine. Please be safe."

When the door closed behind him, she dead bolted it. Then she turned on the television. She had to keep her mind occupied while she waited to speak to Juan. How was she going to assure her son that she would bring him home with Toran there ready to contradict her? She didn't want to upset Juan any more than he already was. And she certainly didn't want to set off Toran. She would have to choose her words carefully during the call.

As Patrick drove onto the interstate in a rental car, he tried to remember any details about Comalcalco that might help him tonight. It was a Maya archaeological site that had been discovered in the late 1800s, and surveying started in 1925. The ancient city had been a center for the production of clay figurines. Comalcalco was constructed of fired clay bricks rather than quarried limestone, which was more common on Maya sites. From what the note said regarding the platform, Patrick would be heading to the area known as the Great Acropolis. He drove, thinking that in another circumstance he would probably find this all fascinating, even exciting, but right now he worried who he might encounter at the site and how he was going to quickly find the information he needed. He had the gun with him, but sure hoped he didn't need to use it.

It was a little after nine when Patrick pulled up to the ruins. Black night surrounded him. If not for the moon's light, the task would be far more difficult. The welcome post was empty, so Patrick could park in the shadows and wait, ensuring no one had followed him. He pulled the car under the canopy of several large trees and lowered the window a few inches, then turned off the engine. A coyote howled in the distance.

Patrick thought about Sonrisa, and how she must be checking the clock until it was time to call Juan. Their kiss had lit a fire inside of him that had been smoldering since they met. Did she feel the same? He thought about calling her to check in but decided against it. He couldn't afford any distractions. Instead, he ran through his plan for the night.

At eleven-thirty, Patrick got out of the car. The night sky gave him some light, and he moved slowly, checking the position of the moon as he went. When he arrived at the spot where he would need to begin measuring his steps, he heard a slight rustling in the nearby shrubbery, then nothing. Hopefully, just an animal. He waited in place for at least a minute and heard nothing more, so he began walking, counting out his steps. He then stopped, turned around, and took forty more paces in the other direction. He kept his eye on the moon's trajectory. When he reached the final step, he listened. Nothing. He pulled his cellphone from his pocket. One minute to midnight. He waited the next sixty seconds, senses on high alert. Then at midnight exactly, he followed the faint light of the moon to the side of the pyramid. From there, he slowly approached, his eye on the spot illuminated by silver light.

When he came to the base of the structure, he pulled out his cellphone and shined the light on the side of the pyramid. It took some time before he noticed an ancient brick near the base that seemed more worn than the others. Getting closer, he studied the area until the light flashed on a symbol inscribed on the old stone. He shot a quick photo, then felt around with one hand on the rough surface. Nothing. He spent another fifteen minutes searching in vain. It looked like the symbol was the extent of his findings tonight.

When he returned to his car, he half expected someone to jump out of the shadows, but it was quiet. He checked the time. It was past twelve now. He wondered how Sonrisa's call with Juan was going. What if something went wrong, he worried. What would she do? He had four hours before he would be back at the hotel to find out.

Sonrisa had set an alarm on her regular cellphone which dinged when it was time to prepare for her call. She went to the wall where she had plugged in the burner phone and pulled it out, her nerves on overdrive at the thought of hearing Toran's voice after all these years. Then she sat down on the bed and took several deep breaths as she picked up the piece of paper on which Patrick had written the phone number. Keeping her fears under control, she opened the burner and pressed the on button, but nothing happened. Panic zinged through her as she pushed the button over and over. Was the phone faulty? Or the wall outlet? She raced into the bathroom and plugged it in there, but still no power. It was midnight. If she didn't call now, she might not get to speak to Juan. Rushing over to the hotel phone, she picked up the receiver and dialed the number. Trying to calm herself, she closed her eyes as the phone started ringing. Please pick up, Toran, she thought.

16

"Well, Andrea," said Toran after the call had rung for what seemed like an eternity. "I finally found the rock you've been hiding under."

"Hello, Toran," Sonrisa said, a knot of fear in her chest triggered by his voice. She had the urge to ask to speak to Juan now but held her tongue. If she began the call demanding, Toran would likely hang up.

"Tell me, Andrea, what was your plan? To raise our son as a Mexican?"

"Toran, I—," Sonrisa started to say she was sorry, but stopped. "May I speak to Callum?"

"Do you really think you deserve to speak to Callum, Little Bird?" he said, using the nickname she had come to despise. "In my mind, you should have to wait a decade before we would be even."

Sonrisa stopped herself from pleading. She knew Toran saw that as weak, and if he saw an opening, he would strike.

"Nothing to say for yourself?"

"Callum has asthma. Did he tell you that? He needs medication."

"Most likely brought on by living in that infernal hellhole of a country. He's fine."

"Is he available?" asked Sonrisa.

"I'll put him on, but only for a minute. You're lucky I've agreed to that."

Sonrisa waited, her heart pounding in her ears.

"No thank you for me, Little Bird?"

Sonrisa grasped the bedspread in one hand, the hate she had for this man scorching through her. "Thank you," she said, keeping her tone even.

"Now was that so difficult?"

Sonrisa didn't respond. After another moment, she heard Toran speaking in a low voice, then Juan said, "Mom."

"Juan, are you okay?"

"I'm fine, but I want to go home."

"I know, sweetie, I'm working on that." She pinched the bridge of her nose to keep from crying.

"He says he's my father and that my real name is Callum," said Juan, sounding confused.

"That's right, he is your father. I'm sorry I didn't tell you the truth, but it's a long story. What have you been doing?"

"He showed me the stable with the horses and ponies. There's one for me named Finley. I'm going to ride him today."

"That sounds like fun," said Sonrisa, relieved he hadn't asked her about his father, the hero. There would be a lot of explaining to do. She ran a hand along her forehead. "You be good, okay? Everything is going to be fine. I love you."

"I love you, too, Mom," said Juan.

There was a brief silence.

"Juan?"

"He's gone to have breakfast."

"Toran, we need to talk about this. Callum can't go without his mother."

86

"From where I sit, he's doing fine without his mother." Then the line went dead.

Sonrisa set the phone on the bed and clasped her hands, trying to steady herself. Speaking with Toran brought up all the feelings of inadequacy she had worked so hard to overcome over the last ten years. He used to make fun of her art and would tell her she wouldn't be able to ever take care of herself or their child. Since she'd been in Mexico, she had proven him wrong. But the moment he said her name, all that self-confidence slipped away.

The drive was long, and fatigue set in around three am for Patrick. He stopped at a gas station to refuel, thankful to find one where the pumps were still operating, despite the station being closed. He stifled a yawn. That was another thing he missed about being in the States. If you were on a road trip in the middle of the night, you could usually find coffee somewhere.

"Mom, Cherie just threw up all over herself," complained Patrick, six at the time. His father was on leave, and they were driving to see his grandparents in Iowa. His baby sister,

Cherie, was two, and it was Patrick's job to keep an eye on her in the back seat.

His mother reached back with a cloth to wipe his sister's mouth.

"Why does she have to be so gross?"

His mother laughed. "That's what babies do. You used to spit up, too. One day, you'll be glad you have a sister. I always wanted a brother or sister."

His dad glanced at him in the rearview mirror and winked. "Your mom is right," he said. "You'll be the oldest, and you can boss her around." His dad laughed when his mom smacked him on the arm.

Patrick looked over at his sister, who gave him a goofy grin. He extended his finger, and she took it and squeezed. "Tighter," Patrick said, crossing his eyes at her. That made her laugh.

His dad had been right. Patrick was happy to have a sister, and later, a brother. But it was he and Cherie who became each other's support systems after their father died. That's what had made the last years so difficult—being away from Cherie, and his mom and Tad. But he would do it all again to protect them.

Patrick pulled up at the hotel a couple of hours before sunrise. He yawned as he made his way to the room. He was about to slip the keycard into the lock when he heard Sonrisa speaking. She sounded agitated, but after listening for a few moments, he didn't hear any other voices. Some more loud words, then it became silent. He opened the door a crack. Quiet. He went inside to find Sonrisa asleep in her bed. He dead bolted the door and slipped out of his clothing, sliding into his bed. She lay facing toward him, and in the dim light he could see her face, now peaceful. What had she been dreaming about, he wondered? There was so much he didn't know about her.

When Patrick awoke a few hours later, sunlight lit up the room, and the smell of coffee and eggs filled the air.

"Good morning," Sonrisa greeted him. She was sitting at the table eating. "I got you some coffee and breakfast."

Patrick sat up and stretched. "It smells fantastic. Is it still morning?"

"Eleven-thirty."

He got out of bed, suddenly remembering he had nothing on but his underwear. He looked at Sonrisa, who eyed his body, then caught his gaze for a moment, finally looking away.

Patrick went to his backpack and pulled out some sweats and put them on, then sat down at the table. "*Huevos rancheros*. Looks good." He took a big bite and washed it down with coffee.

"Did you get what you needed last night?" asked Sonrisa.

Patrick finished chewing a mouthful. "Yes, although I need to decipher it. What about you? Did you have your phone call with Juan?"

Sonrisa set down her coffee cup. "I did."

When she didn't expound, Patrick asked, "Is Juan okay?"

She picked up a piece of toast, then put it back down. "He sounded okay. Toran is spoiling him. He's already given him a pony."

Patrick took a sip of coffee. "That's good news, isn't it? That he's treating him well."

Sonrisa nodded. "Yes, of course. But now that Toran has him, I don't know how I'll ever get him back."

Patrick buttered his toast and spread it with jelly. "We should be hearing from the American Embassy soon. Try to stay positive."

"It's hard after talking to Toran."

"Did he threaten you in any way?"

"Not directly. He just..." Sonrisa pushed her hair away from her face. "He has a way of threatening me where someone listening wouldn't notice it. Like his nickname for me."

"What is it?"

"Little Bird. It sounds innocent enough, but he goes grouse hunting, and especially enjoys the kill. He took me hunting one time and tried to get me to shoot grouse, but I wouldn't. Then for the next two hours I had the displeasure of seeing how much he loved to shoot them out of the sky. From then on, he called me Little Bird."

"What a charmer," said Patrick. "The burner phone worked well?"

"Actually, I couldn't get it to charge."

Patrick was about to take a sip of coffee but stopped. "How did you call? Not with your cellphone?"

Sonrisa shook her head. "I used the hotel phone."

"Sonrisa! He could have people on their way here now."

"I know I was to only use the burner phone, but I couldn't miss what could be the only opportunity to speak to my son. I'm sorry. I didn't know what else to do."

Patrick put down his toast and pushed his food away. "If they show up, it's for one reason. To kill you." He stood. "C'mon, we're getting out of here."

17

"I know Toran," Sonrisa protested. "He might have manhandled me, but he's not a killer."

Patrick gave Sonrisa a hard look. "Do you really want to take that chance? If he gets rid of you, he has Juan all to himself."

That last statement made Sonrisa pause. He was right, she couldn't chance it. She started gathering her things.

A couple minutes later, they headed out, Patrick taking the stairs down to the parking lot two steps at a time.

"I got a rental car." Patrick pointed at a Hyundai.

They hurried over, and as Sonrisa buckled herself in, she looked up at the balcony. In front of their room were two men. "Oh, my God." She quickly turned her head away.

Patrick glanced up, then started the car. "Get down on the floor," he said. "I'm going to drive out slowly."

Sonrisa took another look up to see one of the men throwing his body against the hotel door. Heart in her throat, she crouched on the floor of the passenger side, quivering as she wrapped her arms around her legs. She began to pray then. The last thing she wanted was to leave her son to grow up under the influence of Toran.

Patrick pulled onto the busy street, the adrenaline from their narrow escape coursing through his veins. He checked the rearview mirror. No one following them. After a couple of miles between them and the hotel, he said, "You can sit up now."

Sonrisa rose and secured her seatbelt. "I'm sorry for putting you in harm's way. I should have known Toran had an ulterior motive when he agreed to let me talk with Juan."

Patrick made a right, then headed east on interstate 180. After driving for several minutes in silence, he said, "I'd make sure your regular cellphone is turned off."

Sonrisa fished the phone out of her purse and checked it. As she did so, Patrick could see her hands shaking.

"We'll get Juan back," he assured her as he sped up the car.

"What about your mission?"

"We'll do both."

Patrick could feel Sonrisa's eyes on him. "I'm not sure what I did to deserve your help," she said, "but I'm grateful for it."

Patrick changed lanes. "Every good person is deserving of help, and you're a good person, Sonrisa. Actually, one of the best people I've ever met." What he didn't say was that he wanted to be by her side for whatever she needed because he had come to care for her. That without being near her every day, his life would seem empty.

. . .

An hour later, they exited the road in Campeche.

"I've heard of this city," said Sonrisa. "It has a port, doesn't it?"

"Well, then, let's find a hotel next to the ocean," said Patrick.

He noticed out of the corner of his eye Sonrisa smiling for the first time that day. He felt glad for something to lighten the mood.

Patrick pulled up to the first big hotel he saw, a multi-story affair with a sweeping front entrance lined with potted palms. He stopped the car. "Wait here. It's probably best we avoid being seen together. Toran's people could be looking for a couple."

When Patrick walked out of the hotel, his stride was quick and determined. He got behind the wheel and handed Sonrisa two keycards. "We have a suite on the tenth floor." Then he turned the car on and headed into the parking garage. When they'd parked, Sonrisa asked, "Should we go in separately?"

Patrick glanced through the windshield and around the garage. "It looks pretty clear, and we're going to take the elevator to our floor, so I think we'll be okay. Anything seems strange, get out and go to our room. Lock yourself in. I'll keep going to the next floor and take the stairs back down."

When they got to the room, Sonrisa slid a keycard in and pushed the door open while Patrick brought in their bags. He set them down in the entryway. "They didn't have any rooms with two beds," he said.

"It's lovely here," said Sonrisa, walking through the living room area to look out a set of double doors that led onto a balcony. People lounged below next to a pool with a waterfall, and beyond that the gulf shimmered a hazy blue in the midday sun.

Inside, the walls were painted the most beautiful shade of aquamarine, with flowing white drapes that puddled onto the floor. Just off the room was an ensuite bathroom, its large, deep tub already inviting. In the bedroom, her eye caught a white, silk duvet piled with hordes of fluffy pillows.

Patrick came to stand behind her, putting an arm around her waist. Sonrisa nearly melted at the comfort his doing so brought her. "Thank you," she said. "I don't know what I would have done without you during this."

"You've taken excellent care of Juan all by yourself. He's smart, strong, level-headed. He got all of that from you."

At the sincerity in Patrick's voice, Sonrisa relaxed against him even more, laying her head back on his chest. "That means a great deal."

Patrick kissed the top of her head. "You mean a great deal, Sonrisa."

Without saying a word, she turned to him and put her finger to his lips, as if to hush him. He kissed her fingertip, then turned her palm over and kissed it gently, running his tongue along her lifeline. As he did so, feelings arose in Sonrisa that she thought no longer existed. He kissed her deeply then and without her realizing it, she began to caress his neck, running her fingernails along the back of his head. He took her lower lip between his teeth and bit it lightly, then kissed her even more deeply. Sonrisa fell back slightly with the weight of him, feeling a heat rise in her. His hands stroked her breasts as he whispered, "I want you" in her ear.

She kissed his cheek, his neck, then grazed her mouth against his. At moments, she felt as if she could barely breathe and her skin, her body, even her mind began to burn.

When they moved away from one another, Patrick breathed, "I want to make love to you, Sonrisa. I think you want me?"

Overcome with emotion, she took his hand.

He led her to the bedroom, then sat at the foot of the bed as she stood in front of him. With his fingers, he pushed her blouse up slightly and trailed his tongue across her stomach. Then he ran his fingers along the tops of her panties, making her legs feel weak. But when he reached to unbutton her blouse, panic overtook her, and she cried out, "Stop!"

18

Stunned at the sharp tone of Sonrisa's voice, Patrick froze. "I'm sorry. I thought you..." he trailed off, unsure of what else to say.

Sonrisa held her blouse tight against her chest. "I did. I do. I..." She looked down at the floor. When she looked back up, he saw anguish in her eyes.

It was then that Patrick knew. "I won't ever hurt you, Sonrisa," he said, his voice a gentle whisper.

"I'm sorry, I..." said Sonrisa.

"You don't ever have to apologize to me for this." Patrick took her hands in his.

They stood that way for several long, quiet moments, then Sonrisa moved her hands to her blouse and opened it. She unclasped her bra and pushed it and the blouse off her shoulders. Patrick hesitantly searched her eyes for confirmation, then he slowly turned her around and gently kissed the scars slashed across her back.

When Patrick kissed the marks Toran had left permanently on her flesh, something shifted in Sonrisa. Unable to stop herself, she cried softly. It was as if the shame she had been carrying around the past several years suddenly washed away. Patrick turned her around and put his lips to hers, then ran one hand lightly over her breasts and kissed the side of her neck.

In response, Sonrisa pulled Patrick's shirt over his head, revealing his broad, muscular chest. Then she unbuttoned his jeans and took his penis in her hands. She stroked until his breath grew deep. When he began panting, he stopped and whispered, "Let's lie down on the bed."

Sonrisa let Patrick guide her to the bed, where he tossed the decorative pillows across the room, then pulled the covers and sheet back. In an instant, he picked her up by the waist and tossed her on the bed, both of them laughing. She loved the playfulness of Patrick, how making love was full of love and caring. He took his time loving her, discovering every inch of her, and giving himself to her in every way possible. Sonrisa had never known such caring, so much giving. And when finally, he opened her legs, she moaned with a depth of desire she never knew existed. He balanced his weight on one arm and entered her slowly, then deeply, pulling back in order to appreciate the sensuality between them. Then he placed a hand beneath her buttocks and as he lifted her to him, plunged into her, loving her until her muscles tightened beneath him.

When Patrick lay to one side and their breathing had steadied, he said, "Thank you for trusting me."

Sonrisa leaned up on one elbow to face him. She stroked his lips with her fingers. "I didn't know if I would ever trust enough for this."

Patrick pulled her close. They lay that way for some time, legs entwined with one another as the late afternoon slipped to evening. At one point, her head on his chest looking out the window, Sonrisa said, "The sunset is incredible."

Patrick stretched. "Let's go out on the balcony and enjoy it. I'll call room service and order a bottle of champagne."

Sonrisa sat up and smiled. "I love that idea." She scooted from the bed and pulled on a slim, dark green dress that fell to her calves. Then she braided her hair in one long braid, letting it hang down her back.

As Patrick got on the phone, he watched Sonrisa dress, then go to the balcony doors and throw them open. He could see that she seemed lighter now, and that made him happy.

Before long, there was a rap on the door, and a waiter appeared with a cart of appetizers, champagne, and an assortment of fresh, tropical fruits.

"You need anything else, *Señor?*"

"I'll call," said Patrick, tipping the waiter generously. He wheeled the cart out to the balcony, where Sonrisa was leaning on the railing admiring the dark fuchsia sky over the water.

"It's all so gorgeous," she said. "It makes me want to paint."

"You should," he said.

"I didn't bring my paints."

"There's a pencil and notepad by the phone," he suggested.

Sonrisa turned to him and grinned, then went into the room and came back with the pad and paper. She sat down and began drawing. When Patrick tried to peek, she shielded the drawing with her hands. "No looking until I'm done," she said.

"Fine, but don't blame me if I eat all of the food." He grabbed a crab cake and piled it high with tartar sauce. As he ate, he watched out of the corner of his eye as Sonrisa worked, her expression intent.

Finally, when the sun was submerged in the gulf, she announced, "It's done." She held the notepad against her cheek.

"Are you going to show me, or do I have to snatch it from you?" said Patrick playfully.

"Patience," she said. Then she turned it around, and Patrick felt a warm sense of amazement come over him. She had drawn him sitting at the table, the sunset at his back.

When he didn't say anything, Sonrisa frowned. "You don't like it?"

Patrick took the notepad from her hands. "I love it," he said. "No one has ever drawn me before. Thank you."

Sonrisa took the bottle of champagne from the ice and opened it, then poured them both a generous glass. She picked hers up. "What shall we toast to?"

"To finding one another in the midst of all this," suggested Patrick.

Sonrisa smiled and touched her glass to Patrick's, then took a long sip.

They sat on the balcony talking as twilight turned to night. Patrick spoke of his family, and what he remembered of his father.

"Your sister, Cherie, sounds wonderful," said Sonrisa. "I always wished I had a sister. I love my brother, Keith, but it would have been so fun to have someone to try on makeup with and braid each other's hair."

"Cherie will like you," he said.

Silence settled between them for a while, then Sonrisa asked, "Do you have to go out tonight?"

"I'm waiting on another message first."

"How will they find you? Haven't you gone off script since we ran from Toran's men?"

Patrick shook his head. "Somehow, they always find me. I'm not concerned."

Sonrisa sighed, and Patrick could see her mood dipping.

"Are you thinking about Juan?" he said.

"Yes." She pushed her champagne glass around in a circle on the table. "While I don't think Toran's intention is to hurt Juan, I'm concerned about Toran influencing him and teaching him to be a terrible person."

"That's not possible," said Patrick. "You raised him too well. Is there anyone in Toran's family who you were close to? Anyone who might help you?"

Sonrisa glanced out at the now dark sky. "Toran's younger brother, Evan. They despise one another. Mainly because Evan is not anything like his brother. Toran was always jealous of Evan, because he was their mother's favorite."

"Do you think you could trust him?"

Sonrisa took a bite of melon. "Though there's no love lost between them, Toran has more power in the family."

"So, Evan's fate is in Toran's hands, so to speak?"

"Exactly."

Patrick scooped up what was left of the ceviche with a cracker. "I've found that when people are pushed down long enough, they tend to finally explode at one point, and, if given an opportunity, will strike back."

"You think I should pit Evan against his brother? But what ammunition could I give him?"

"The necklace in your house in Veracruz."

19

Sonrisa thought about Patrick's suggestion. Would Evan help her with Juan? Or was he still afraid of his older brother?

"It's worth a try," she said. "But I have no idea how to get ahold of him."

"I'll text Lance at Interpol and see if he can get us a cell-phone number," said Patrick, picking up his phone.

"Before you do, Evan's last name is Suelo," she said.

"A different nationality?"

"Yes, Filipino. Another reason for Toran's disdain."

Patrick punched in the request, then opened the photo of the symbol he had taken the night before.

"This symbol was on the pyramid last night. But I can't make heads or tails of it, to be honest," he said.

She reached for his phone. "May I?"

Patrick handed it over.

Sonrisa looked more closely. "It resembles antlers," she said. "It appears to be an emblem of some sort. Does it bother you, not knowing all the pieces of the puzzle as to what you're working on right now?"

Patrick shrugged his shoulders. "If it gets me home, then

I'm fine with it. When I was working back in Jersey, I thought I knew what I was doing, but in the end there was something else going on."

"What will you do when you go home?"

"To start," said Patrick, "I'll be very, very grateful." He smiled a bittersweet smile.

"Your absence must be so hard for your mother," said Sonrisa, worry about Juan welling up in her at the thought.

"That's something I've felt bad about every day since I've been here," said Patrick.

"Do you think Toran's men will be able to track us down?"

"Though you've been keeping your phone off, we don't know if they are aware you're with me. We have to be extra careful."

Just then his phone buzzed, and he checked the screen. "I've got a number for Evan. It's nearly six in the morning in Scotland."

"From what I remember, he gets up early, so I could call him," said Sonrisa. "I don't know if that burner phone works."

"Let me try."

Sonrisa got it out of her bag along with the charger and handed them to Patrick.

After looking at it for a moment, he said, "They gave us the wrong charger. Mine might work." He got up and matched the plugs, and the phone started to charge. "Give it a few minutes, then you should have enough juice to call him."

"What should I say?" asked Sonrisa.

"You have one goal, and that's to get Juan. Let Evan know you'll do whatever it takes—within reason—to get him back. If he isn't sounding amenable, tell him about the necklace, but don't tell him where it is."

Sonrisa nodded, then went over to the phone. "There's already a five percent charge. I'm going to call."

Patrick came to stand beside her and showed her the number from Lance. Her heart did a flip-flop at the thought of speaking to another person she thought she had left in the past.

"Put it on speaker phone, if that's okay," said Patrick.

She nodded.

After several rings, a voice answered. "Hello?"

"Evan, it's me, Andrea."

She heard an intake of breath on the other end of the phone. "Andrea, you shouldn't be calling me."

"I'm sorry. I don't want to put you in the middle with Toran, but I need to talk to you about Callum. Do you know what your brother has done?"

There was silence for a moment, then he said, "Some would say he just took back what is his."

"People aren't possessions," said Sonrisa. "I thought you would understand that."

"I do understand," he said. "What I don't understand is why you didn't at least get word to me that you were both okay all this time."

"I'm sorry, Evan. I just wasn't sure how without compromising my whereabouts."

She heard him breathing steadily on the other end of the phone. "Why are you calling me now?"

"I need your help getting Callum back."

"I can't go against my brother. You know that."

Sonrisa felt tears heating up the back of her eyes. She balled her fist against the side of her leg. "My son is my entire world," she said. "He needs to be with me. I thought maybe you could speak with your mother. Surely, she would understand."

"She might have, but she passed last year. That's something you would have known had you stayed in touch."

"Evan, I'm so sorry," said Sonrisa.

"I'm sorry that you are separated from your son, but my hands are tied."

"What if I help you untie them?"

"And how would you do that?"

"I have something that belongs to the family," she said.

"So, it was you who took the necklace."

"Yes." Sonrisa bit her lower lip.

"Toran suspected a maid who worked at the house. He had her beaten for information about its whereabouts."

Sonrisa gasped. "Oh, no! Is she okay?"

Evan was silent. "I need to hang up now, Andrea."

"Evan, please, don't. If you help me get Callum back, I'll give you the necklace."

There was more silence on the other end of the phone. "You still have it?"

Patrick got Sonrisa's attention by putting a finger to his lips.

"I know where it is," she said. "If you help me secure my boy, I will gladly give it to you."

"I have your word?"

"You have my word."

Evan didn't say anything for a minute. "Let me figure out logistics. I'll be in touch."

"Thank you, Evan," said Sonrisa, but by the time the words had left her lips, the line was dead.

She looked at Patrick. "What do you think?"

Patrick kept her gaze for a long time before speaking. "You didn't tell me Toran's brother is in love with you."

20

Sonrisa looked like she was about to protest, then said, "I don't know about love, but he did seem to care for me. One night, he even promised to get me away from Toran."

"What happened?" asked Patrick.

"We were out in the garden and he told me he couldn't bear to see me beaten anymore. But Toran found out from the family driver about our conversation. Like I said, he is paranoid and has spies everywhere. He was so angry. He and Evan got in a terrible fight."

"How do you know that Evan won't go straight to Toran with this?"

"I don't know for sure, but their rivalry runs deep. Now with their mother gone, it must be even worse for Evan. If I can give him the necklace, that may give him the power and control he's been looking for."

"Well, if Evan does agree to help you, I'd suggest proceeding with great caution. His emotions for you may cloud his otherwise reliable judgement."

The night Patrick and Nick headed out for the gas station job, the tension was thick. Finally, Patrick asked, "Is something up with Frankie?"

Nick spit on the sidewalk as they made their way to an alley near the station. "He found out Suzette has been cheating on him with Paulo Ricci."

"I've heard that name."

"He's with the Brothers. A lieutenant now. The tall, blonde, and handsome type, like you. Frankie is so mad he's spitting bullets. I'd advise only speaking when spoken to."

Nick stopped walking and turned to face Patrick. "Enough about the boss. You remember what we talked about? This goes like it's supposed to, and your mother can buy a new car." He pulled two ski masks out of his jacket and handed one to Patrick.

Patrick took the mask, the unsettled feeling in his gut he'd been walking around with for months heavier than usual. "Why are we hitting a gas station, anyway? They couldn't have more than five grand."

Nick cracked his knuckles. "We just do what we're told and don't worry about the rest." He slapped Patrick on the shoulder. "Now let's go."

Patrick hesitated, then followed.

"You looked like you were far away just now," said Sonrisa.

"No, just tired," said Patrick. "How about we get some sleep?"

As Sonrisa got ready for bed, Patrick checked his messages for next steps but there was no news.

A few minutes later, they climbed into bed and Patrick pulled Sonrisa close to him. As she scooted up against his chest, he kissed the top of her head. She smelled like soap, her hair still damp from the shower. He loved Sonrisa's gentleness, and he wished he would never have to let her go. In his life, things often changed unexpectedly, and people left. He wasn't sure what tomorrow would bring, but he was definitely enjoying this moment with her.

Early the next morning, Patrick awoke to an unfamiliar sound. He jumped out of bed and saw a manila envelope lying on the entryway floor. He picked it up and brought it over to the table.

Sitting down, he unclasped the envelope and pulled out a piece of parchment paper. He flattened it on the table and read: *Put your ear to the ground to find on the furthermost corner of a tall pyramid a large crack, within which lies a crypt. When you have traveled fifty meters within, you will come to an underground spring. The treasure lies beneath the spring. You will know it from the emblem it displays. Bring the object to us, and your life will be renewed. You have twenty-four hours before the offer becomes void.*

Patrick read the message several times. Where was this pyramid with the crypt? He reached for his backpack and pulled out the map he had been preparing over the last several months. He unfolded it and set it on the table, then put a finger on where he'd been last. But there was no telling from this message where he would go next. There were thousands of Maya ruins in Mexico.

Patrick got up and put on a pot of coffee, his mind spinning. He had just one day to find whatever they wanted him to find, or what? Go back to his cabin in Puerto Vallarta? He couldn't have come this far not to finish the task and make it home. He began to feel trapped, and it made him angry. Angry at what occurred all those years ago to get him into this mess and angry now at the people pulling his strings.

When Sonrisa put her hand on his shoulder, he jumped slightly. He was so used to living alone that he had, for a moment, forgotten she was there.

"Everything okay?"

"Did you want some coffee?" he asked as he poured himself a cup.

"I'll take some," she said. "I see the map on the table. Is that new?"

Patrick handed her a cup and took his to the table. "A new missive that's even more unclear than before."

Sonrisa came to stand beside him and read the message. "What if you don't find the item they want in time?"

"Then I forfeit the opportunity to go home."

21

"Put your ear to the ground," read Patrick out loud from the message he had received. "For some reason, that keeps jumping out at me. I wonder if it's literal."

Sonrisa pointed to the line about a spring. "Which ruins have nearby lakes or rivers?"

Patrick flipped through a notebook, then stopped. "One is Chichen Itza. If I recall, another one is also in the Yucatán Peninsula." He flipped a few more pages. "The Coba Ruins located in the jungle, and the least excavated of all the ruins. They say there are still five thousand mounds to be unearthed and discovered." Patrick put his head in his hands. "I will never figure this out."

Sonrisa pulled out a chair and sat down. "They wouldn't have given you this task if they didn't think you could do it." She put her hand on his. "I'll help you."

"What about Juan?"

"At the moment, I can't do anything about Juan. This will keep my mind occupied. You'd be doing me a favor."

They spent the next couple of hours scouring every-thing they could find online and in his notes. Both sites were of historical significance, and both had underground springs.

"I'm leaning toward the Coba Ruins," said Patrick. "The site is located near four lakes, which is rare in Yucatán. And the city had fifty thousand people living there at its peak."

Sonrisa leaned over to read the note again when Patrick's phone rang.

"It's the American Embassy," he said. "I'll put it on speaker."

"Hello," said Sonrisa, putting a hand to her chest.

"Is this Andrea Black?"

"Yes."

"My name is Heidi Monroe, and I've been assigned to your case."

"It's a case now?"

Heidi paused. "Yes, it is considered a kidnapping on both sides of the borders now."

Sonrisa's face was tense. "What does that mean?"

"It means this is a tricky diplomatic situation that unfortunately won't be resolved overnight. I'm going to need more information from you to sort this out. Juan was taken two nights ago in Veracruz, correct?"

"Yes, he was forcibly taken from his bed in the early morning hours."

"And have you spoken to him since then?"

"I did," said Sonrisa. "Last night."

"Did your son at that time express being in danger?"

"Well, no," said Sonrisa. "But he's definitely not happy about being there. He asked to go home. He's just a little boy."

"I understand," said Heidi. "And I am not asking these questions to upset you."

Sonrisa leaned closer to the phone. "One thing of note, my son has asthma and doesn't have his medication with him."

"That is something," said Heidi. "Did you mention this to Mr. Murray?"

"I did, and he dismissed my concerns and said my son was fine." Sonrisa's voice broke.

"Okay, I know this is much easier said than done, but please try to remain calm. I'm going to do everything in my power to get your boy back."

"Thank you," said Sonrisa. "Is there anything I should do now?"

"Stay available. If I'm able to arrange for Juan's transport out of Scotland, where our sources say he was last seen, I will need you to act quickly."

"I can do that," said Sonrisa, sitting up straighter.

When Heidi hung up, Sonrisa said, "At this point, we don't even know if Juan is still in Scotland."

"When you hear from Evan, you can ask him," said Patrick.

"I've thought about what you said. It's been several years. I have no idea if Evan is now in allegiance with his brother. If that's the case, I may not hear from him."

"That family necklace will be irresistible to him."

"For Juan's sake, I hope you're right," said Sonrisa.

Patrick felt frustrated from all sides. Sonrisa was no closer to being reunited with Juan, and now he only had twenty-three hours left to find and deliver the antiquity, whatever and wherever it was.

Sonrisa pushed her hair back, then picked up the map. "For now, there's nothing else I can do about Juan," she said, almost to herself. "How far apart are the two ruins?"

"Close to one another, but I don't have enough time to go back and forth," said Patrick. "I need to choose the right one first."

"Then go with your gut," said Sonrisa.

"Just do as I told you," said Nick when they were close to the gas station. "I'll get the guy to open the safe. All you need to do is be on the lookout. Anyone tries to come in, do something to stop them."

Patrick felt his blood pumping in his ears. This was real now. Suddenly, he didn't want to continue. He stopped walking.

Nick was a few paces ahead of him and swung around. "What's your problem?"

"I don't think I can do this," said Patrick.

Nick's face turned to stone as he advanced on Patrick. "You're going to do this, you hear?" he growled. "Frankie is depending on you. And remember, we know where your mom and kid sister and brother live."

"You're threatening my family?" asked Patrick, a ball of fury suddenly blinding him. He clenched both hands into fists.

"I haven't put all this work into training you for no reason. We gotta get this over with, now."

"Why the hurry?" Patrick threw his head back defiantly.

Nick grabbed him by the shirt and pulled him close, spittle raining on his face when he said, "Stop your back talk." Then he let go of Patrick's shirt and laughed. "Don't worry about it. Soon you'll be home giving your mother a wad of cash."

2 2

When they were ready to head out for the ruins, Sonrisa gave Patrick a bright smile. "Let's go find a treasure."

"I like it when you do that," said Patrick, reaching out and pulling her close to him.

Sonrisa raised her eyebrows. "Do what?"

"Smile."

She ran a fingertip across his brow. "How about a smile from you?"

"How about a kiss to make me smile?" said Patrick.

Sonrisa laughed. "We don't have time."

"For a kiss?"

She giggled. "Okay, fine." Then she pecked him on the cheek and grabbed her purse, checking her reflection in the mirror. She had dressed for hiking in jeans and a yellow T-shirt, her hair pulled back in a bright green bandana.

Once in the car headed toward the ruins, Sonrisa thought about Juan. Would the embassy be able to do anything? As if sensing her thoughts, Patrick reached over and rubbed her shoulder. Moved by the gesture of affection, she put her hand on his. They drove that way for a while, Sonrisa filled with an intimate emotion she hadn't felt before. To have a man genuinely care about her, without demanding, that was something she had never experienced.

"About my scars," she said suddenly, surprising herself at speaking up about it.

Patrick glanced over, a pained look on his face. "You don't need to talk about that."

She felt the warmth of his hand, courage welling up in her. "I feel like I do."

Patrick looked at her again, then back at the road. "I'm listening."

"That's the thing. You do listen," said Sonrisa. "You hear me. I don't think I've ever experienced that before, except maybe through my art."

Patrick glanced in the rearview mirror, then back at the road. "I can understand that."

"My father wasn't a nice man. He was controlling and demanding of my mother," she said. "He was also very strict with my brother and me. Keith got the brunt of things, including beatings. He struggled with a lot of expectations because he was older, and a boy. My father would boss me around, then otherwise ignore me. I think I thought that's what normal was, so when Toran came along and lavished me with attention and gifts, I felt like my prince charming had arrived, and I fell for his ruse. I know it's no excuse for letting him hurt me, but—" She looked out the window. "I just need you to understand."

Patrick shocked Sonrisa by removing his hand from hers and pulling over to the side of the road. He turned to her. "I don't for a minute believe you let Toran do anything to you," he said, his tone firm. "He took advantage of you and abused you, Sonrisa. Those scars are all him. All you did was give your trust where it wasn't deserved."

Sonrisa looked at Patrick, struggling for a response.

Finally, she said, "Thank you. I've worked to forgive myself for putting up with him hurting me. But you're right, it was all him. Now I just need to believe that."

Patrick's face softened. "I'm sorry if I raised my voice."

Sonrisa shook her head. "I needed to hear that."

Patrick pulled back onto the road. "There is no way that man is going to raise your son."

They pulled into Coba in midafternoon when the sun was still bright. Before they could park, Patrick had to pay an attendant, who then waved them into a spot in the shade.

After he shut off the car, Patrick said, "From my research of this ruin, it takes a good two to three hours to explore the area, so we better get moving."

They got out of the car and walked to the entrance where a Mexican man stood in a wooden kiosk. He smiled widely and said, "*Buenos tardes.* Five dollars each, please."

Patrick pulled some bills from his pocket and handed them to the man, who gave them a black and white map of the ruins.

They stood under the shade of a tree to examine the map. "I'm betting on the area over here near this lake," said Patrick, pointing. "There's a tall pyramid there, too, which the note mentions. If we take this route, we can get a panoramic view."

Sonrisa glanced up at the bright blue sky studded with clouds as they started down the path. After only a few yards into the jungle, Sonrisa heard Patrick's phone ringing. He stopped and pulled it out, checking the screen. "It's the embassy."

Sonrisa could feel her heart racing as she took the phone from Patrick. "Hello?"

"Ms. Black, this is Heidi Monroe with the American

Embassy. There has been a new development regarding your son."

Sonrisa felt her stomach tighten and chewed her bottom lip.

"Mr. Murray has petitioned the court in Scotland demanding a paternity test."

"Why? He knows Juan is his son."

"He is saying there is a possibility that his brother is the father."

Sonrisa felt like screaming. "That's ludicrous."

"It's possible he is stalling for time," said Heidi. "I can't be sure of his motivation. I do know his father has also been involved in the negotiations."

Sonrisa pressed the phone close to her ear, trying to keep the helplessness she felt from creeping into her tone. "What would you like me to do at this point?"

"Just sit tight. And make sure I can reach you."

Sonrisa let out a breath. "I will, thank you."

The woman was silent for a moment, then added, "I don't have children, but I do have a niece I am close to. If she had been taken like this, I would be very upset. Try to keep your chin up."

When Sonrisa hung up the phone, she said, "That monster is now having Juan go through a paternity test."

"Why do you think he came up with that?"

Sonrisa looked around, at a loss. "Most likely to mess with everyone's heads. Can I have your phone? I want to call Evan."

"Do you think it's a good idea?"

"Heidi told me their father is also involved. That might not be good news for Evan. I owe him that much."

"Is there something more between you and Evan?" asked Patrick.

"I told you nothing happened," Sonrisa said, feeling defensive for the first time with Patrick.

"That's not what I'm talking about," said Patrick. "Evan was the one who arranged for you and Juan to get out of Scotland, wasn't he?"

Sonrisa glanced over Patrick's shoulder, then back into his eyes. "I promised I'd never tell a soul, but yes. If Toran's father ever found out, I don't know what would happen to Evan."

Patrick handed her his phone. "Just be careful what you say."

Sonrisa dialed Evan's number. When he answered with a tentative hello, she said, "It's me."

"I don't have any news," he said. "I'm still working to figure out how to get Callum out safely."

"I'm not calling to push you. I just want to know that he is okay. And I need to tell you what Toran is up to."

"I saw Callum this morning riding his pony. He looked well."

Relief washed through Sonrisa. "Okay, thank you."

"Tell me about Toran."

"Are you sure your phone isn't being tapped?" she asked.

"I had someone check it earlier. I'm clear for the moment, and I'm outside right now."

"Toran is having a paternity test done with Callum."

"But he knows Callum is his."

"I think he's fishing," said Sonrisa.

"For what?"

"You know what."

The silence between them was palpable for a moment, then Evan replied, "That is buried very deep. There is no way he is going to unearth it."

"But can you be certain? We both know that if he finds out you helped me, he'll..."

Evan finished her sentence. "Kill me."

"He has already tried to kill me," she said. "Please watch your step with this."

"Will you really give me the necklace?"

"I will."

"Then I'll work something out to get Callum off the estate. Just give me a bit more time."

"How will you do it?"

"It's best for your own safety that you know nothing," he said, then clicked off.

23

"From the look on your face, I can't tell if that was good or bad news."

"I'm not sure." Sonrisa told Patrick about the call.

"I'm going to count that as good," he said. "It sounds like Evan is on your side."

They made their way up the path, which had a gentle ascent at first, then became steeper. After walking for some time, they came to a landing overlooking the jungle floor. The view showed various smaller pyramids amongst the dense greenery, and a larger one in the distance.

"It's gorgeous," said Sonrisa, pulling a water bottle out of her purse. She opened it and took a few long drinks, then handed it to Patrick. The sun was hot, but a good breeze was blowing.

He took the bottle and surveyed the land below. "It is beautiful." Then he noticed that one corner of the large pyramid was much greener than the others. He pulled out his binoculars and looked closer. Could they have found the location with the underground water source?

"Anything?" asked Sonrisa.

Patrick handed her the binoculars and pointed. "Look at the corner of the larger pyramid."

Sonrisa peered through the binoculars, then lowered them. "It is much greener in that area." She glanced at him. "You're thinking there is an underground spring there?"

"I wonder how we get down there."

Just then a man who looked like he worked at the ruins came walking down the path. "*Perdóname,* do you work here?" Patrick asked him.

The man stopped and smiled, adjusting the garbage bags in his hands. "*Sí.*"

Patrick pointed to the base of the pyramid. "How do we get down there?"

The man shook his head. "It is blocked off."

"Why?"

He shrugged. "*No sé.*"

Patrick thanked the man, then continued studying the area below. "I think if we keep heading up, there will be a spot where we are alongside the larger pyramid," he said.

"You heard the man. It's closed off."

Patrick winked at her. "Good thing we wore our hiking boots."

Sonrisa looked down at her sneakers, then chuckled. "Good thing."

They continued another few minutes on the path until they were across from the large pyramid. Sonrisa pointed under the railing to what looked like a path. "I think we can make our way down from there."

They waited until there were no witnesses, then slipped under the railing. Then they began making their way down the steep slope, sliding at times, holding onto thick jungle vines as they went.

"I used to play in the woods when I was a kid with my brother," said Sonrisa. "We'd find wild raspberry bushes growing in the forest and stuff ourselves with the fruit, becoming covered in red."

"That sounds like a great memory," said Patrick, reaching his hand up for Sonrisa and helping her over a clump of vegetation. He saw her arms were getting scratched. "I should have told you to wear long sleeves."

"I've had much worse. As a kid, I used to come home with cuts and bruises all the time. I'm a lot tougher than I look."

After what seemed like a long time, they finally made it to the bottom of the hill. The pyramid lay in the distance. "It looks like the way from here is fairly clear," said Patrick.

Just then, a noise sounded in the nearby brush. Sonrisa yelped as something ran by her legs and made its way to the other side of the path. "An iguana." She laughed.

Patrick knew of the many animals that could be here in the jungle and counted them lucky it was just an iguana. But he didn't want to alarm Sonrisa. Instead, he said, "We should keep our eyes peeled for birds. I hear there are Ocellated Turkeys and Altamira Orioles here. Both quite colorful."

It was warm and Patrick was sweating from their climb. He took a handkerchief out of his backpack and handed it to Sonrisa, who wiped her brow, then he did the same. He checked the sky, noting that the sun had started to dip. It was probably past four by now.

"We better get to the pyramid. We're starting to run out of daylight," he said.

When they arrived at the foot of the pyramid, Sonrisa glanced up at the large structure, then looked at Patrick. "I've got a good feeling about this."

"Feeling that we've found the right pyramid?"

"Yes, but first," she opened her purse, "I grabbed some

pretzels and nuts from the hotel store before we left. Let's rest a minute and have some." She pulled the snacks from her bag, then opened the nuts and poured some into Patrick's hand. "Mm," she said as she crunched on the nuts. "I'm really hungry, aren't you?"

He nodded, putting part of the nuts into his mouth.

Once they finished eating, they began searching the corner of the pyramid where the lush vegetation grew. After an hour of pushing past vines to no avail, Patrick had begun to think they had chosen the wrong pyramid, when Sonrisa called out, "I've found something."

He walked over to where she stood examining a crack that started at the base of the pyramid and rose about three feet in the shape of an oval. He pushed against the crack, but it seemed solid.

"We would need dynamite to get inside," he said.

"Try hitting it with the tire iron you packed," suggested Sonrisa.

Patrick got out the iron and hit the pyramid a few times. "I'm pretty sure the Mexican authorities would throw us in jail for desecrating sacred property," he said.

"I'll keep watch," said Sonrisa.

Patrick began to hit around the perimeter of the oval as hard as he could, and at one point, the crack deepened. He stopped and got on his hands and knees. With the edge of the tire iron, he began working around the crack. The now-loosened stone began to drop away. When he had passed around the entire perimeter, he pressed, and the stone crumbled inward. By now, the sun was setting, and darkness was closing in around them.

"I think we might be in." Heart hammering from the exertion, Patrick stopped to rest for a moment, then peered into the crevice, which was black inside. He put his hand through the opening and felt cool air, then listened. He heard the trickle of water.

Patrick and Sonrisa spent the next hour clearing away the stone rubble in front of the opening, taking turns shining a flashlight as they went. Finally, they had a path in. He took the flashlight and lit up the dark interior. Now that he'd found the location he'd been moving toward all this time, he suddenly felt frozen in place. He glanced back at the now-dark sky, studded with stars.

"Should we go in?" asked Sonrisa.

Patrick hesitated. "I'm not sure what lies inside. It could be dangerous."

Sonrisa glanced into the black night. "It could also be dangerous out here. I say we go in."

"I'll go first." Patrick crawled through the opening and shined the flashlight around, finding himself in a small cavern. "Come in," he said.

Sonrisa came inside and crouched beside him. The space was only about four feet high and six feet wide. He pushed on a wall. It was moist but solid.

Patrick illuminated the back of the cavern to see there was a narrow passageway. "The note said to go fifty meters back, which is a little more than fifty yards."

He got on his hands and knees and led the way down the passageway. As they continued, the air became moister. Patrick heard water dripping more loudly now. They came around a bend then, and he illuminated the area to see water trickling out of the side of the wall, creating a pool in the center of the space.

"I think we found it," said Patrick, excitement beginning to course through his veins. He crawled into the opening, which had more overhead clearance and stood, the top of his head brushing against the stone ceiling.

Sonrisa came in after him.

Patrick took a small shovel out of his backpack and handed the pack to Sonrisa. He stuck the shovel into various areas of the puddle. Nothing. Then he looked at the wall. It said under the spring. He began sliding the shovel against the wall, working his way across. Suddenly, the shovel hit something hard.

24

"Did you find something?" asked Sonrisa, her voice echoing in the musty space.

"It could just be a rock," said Patrick, kneeling and shoveling away the soil from the side of the wall. Then he reached in and felt around with his fingers. It didn't feel like stone. He could swear it was metal. "I think I've got something." He grabbed the shovel again and pushed it into the soil deeper, then pulled back and forth to loosen the earth. He worked steadily and carefully. The object was old and could easily break into pieces.

Suddenly, the metal piece loosened from the earth, and he reached in to pull it out. Before long, he held what looked like a medallion.

"Is that what they're looking for?" asked Sonrisa, shining the light on Patrick's find. "Maybe it's a talisman meant for protection."

"They've never actually told me—just that the item is priceless." He turned it over. "It looks valuable."

Patrick wiped the wet earth away from the face of the medallion. "What I haven't been able to figure out is why whoever has been giving me the clues doesn't just come here himself or herself."

"Maybe they couldn't for some reason. Perhaps the risk was too great," said Sonrisa. "It wasn't easy to get in here."

Patrick checked the ground for any more items, and when he didn't find anything, slid the medallion into his pocket. "Are you ready to head out? It's going to be hard to make it back up the hill in the dark. We do have the flashlight."

When they got to the mouth of the cave, Patrick shined the flashlight outside. He spotted something several yards away. He shut off the flashlight and slowly backed into the cavern.

"What's the matter?" asked Sonrisa.

"I'm pretty sure I just saw a jaguar out near the tree line."

"Oh, my God," said Sonrisa. She reached over and grabbed Patrick's arm. "What do we do?"

"We stay put. If the animal tries to explore the cavern, I'll shoot it." He pulled the gun out of his backpack and took off the safety.

As she crouched in the small space watching the opening to the cavern and the dark night beyond, Sonrisa's heart hammered in her ears. What was she thinking agreeing to this escapade? If she were to die out here mauled by a wild animal, Juan would have to stay with Toran, and he'd never know what happened to his mother.

"I'm sorry," said Patrick. "I think it's best we stay here for the night. Once day breaks, we'll be a lot safer." He pulled a sweatshirt from his backpack and put it on the ground facing the exit, then motioned for Sonrisa to sit beside him.

She crawled over and sat down, looking warily at the gun in his hands. "Have you ever shot a gun?" she asked. "I mean, I know you did target practice with Estevan, but other than that?"

Patrick looked at the gun. "No, and I'm hoping not to have to." He put his arm around Sonrisa, pulling her close. "Sleep, if you want to. I'll keep watch."

She laid her head against Patrick's broad shoulder but was unable to close her eyes.

Before long, Patrick felt Sonrisa relax against him and her breathing soften. Though they were in less than desirable circumstances, he was happy to have her next to him. There was a calm and ease about being with her that he hadn't experienced with many people. It was as if she didn't have to say anything to him, because she already knew him.

When Patrick and Nick arrived at the gas station, the owner was standing behind the counter putting packets of cigarettes onto the shelves. Nick muttered under his breath, "He's not supposed to be here."

"Maybe we should come back," whispered Patrick.

Nick stopped for a moment and considered, then shook his head. "We go back without what we came for, Frankie will kill us both. This has to happen tonight. Put on the ski mask. We'll make this quick."

Every fiber in Patrick screaming to turn and run the other way, he slid the ski mask on and followed Nick into the gas shop.

When Nick pulled out the gun and started waving it around, the owner said, "What do you want?"

"Don't even think about pushing the alarm," said Nick. "Open the safe. Do what I say, and you won't get hurt."

When the man started to reach under the counter, Nick fired a shot, nearly hitting him. The man backed up, raising his arms, "Okay, the safe is in the back."

Nick pointed the gun at the man and screeched, "Let's go."

The two walked into the back, while Patrick kept watch. He heard Nick shouting from the back room. "Open the safe now. I want everything in there, including the book." More arguing from the man, then Nick became angrier. "I know you have it. Give it to me." Patrick heard struggling, then a gunshot. Seconds later, Nick came running out, pushing Patrick toward the door. "We gotta get out of here."

They were heading for the alley when Nick cried out, "Wait, I dropped something." Patrick stopped in the shadows as Nick ran back into the store, then came racing out, a notebook in his hand.

A car drove up at that moment, and a guy cried through the open window, "Hey, I know you."

Nick shot at him several times, then he and Patrick raced away from the station as the sound of sirens filled the night.

When the light of dawn crept in through the opening in the pyramid, Patrick opened his eyes.

Sonrisa stirred next to him, then sat up. "Juan?"

Patrick put his arm around her. "We're in the pyramid."

She rubbed her face.

"I would ask how you slept, but I'm sure it was as cramped and crummy as me."

Sonrisa screwed up her face. "Did you dream of jaguars dismembering us? I did."

Patrick laughed. "Not that I remember, but I did dream of ancient medallions. Let's take a good look at it now that it's light. He reached into his pocket and pulled out the medallion. "It looks like the symbol on the other pyramid," he said, holding it up and turning it over. Just then he heard voices. He slipped the medallion back into his pocket and crawled to the opening and peered out. Two men were talking up on the overlook and pointing to the pyramid. He turned to Sonrisa. "They must have seen the evidence of our excavation. We need to get out of here."

They waited until the men left the landing, then quickly crawled out of the cavern and ran toward the hill. Then they scrambled up the path, and ran through the ruins unimpeded, until they neared the exit, stopping when they saw two men near the kiosk. One wore a police uniform and was nodding as the other man pointed down the path.

Patrick and Sonrisa ducked into the nearby jungle and waited as the police officer passed. Once he was out of sight, Patrick whispered, "I'm going to create a diversion at the entrance, then we'll run to the car." He picked up a handful of stones, and went to the edge of the path, throwing them in the area across from the kiosk. The man snapped his head around and went to investigate. They took the opportunity to run down the path and out into the parking lot. They were halfway to the car when the man called out, *"Espere!"*

Patrick pulled the keys out of his pants and opened the car, then tossed his things in the back while Sonrisa hopped into the passenger seat. As they backed up and pointed toward the exit, the man came running after them. Patrick floored the car, seeing in the rearview mirror the man stop running to make a phone call. Patrick drove faster.

"As you likely know," said Patrick, "here in Mexico, it's guilty until proven innocent. We want to do everything we can to avoid getting stopped and searched."

Sonrisa turned and glanced back. "If I get arrested with an antiquity, I'll never see Juan again."

Patrick drove in silence for a time, checking the road behind them. Then he said, "We could hide the medallion in the jungle somewhere."

"What about your deadline to deliver it?"

"Juan is more important," he said. "I'll pull over if you want. Just tell me."

25

Sonrisa's heart filled with gratitude at Patrick's words. She glanced back several times, but there were still no cars in the distance. Finally, she said, "Keep going."

An hour later, when there was still no sign of the police, Sonrisa began to relax. "Where are you to deliver the medallion?" she asked.

"Let's see if I've gotten a message," he said, reaching into his pocket and pulling out his cellphone. He glanced at the screen as he drove. "A bunch of messages are coming through right now. Shit, a lot from Heidi at the Embassy."

Panic raced through Sonrisa. "She said to be close in case she called."

"We've got a voicemail," said Patrick, pushing play. *Ms. Black, I have arranged for you to take a flight out to Scotland tomorrow afternoon to retrieve Juan. The condition is that you stay in Scotland to discuss shared custody. Please call me back immediately.*

"When was the call?" Sonrisa asked.

"Yesterday evening. I must not have had reception when we were in the pyramid." He handed her the phone.

Sonrisa dialed Heidi's number, but it went to voicemail. "Heidi, this is Andrea. I apologize for being out of contact last night. You can call me now about the flight out." She put the phone in her lap. "It's still morning," said Sonrisa, more to herself than Patrick. "There's still time to make the flight."

They drove in silence for a time, then Patrick said, "It sounds like good news. Like Heidi made some headway with Toran."

Sonrisa nodded. "Except for the part about shared custody."

Realizing Sonrisa would soon be getting on a plane, Patrick felt a sense of disappointment. Everything in him wanted to go with her to get Juan. His phone pinged then. A message that simply gave coordinates and said: *Delivery, seven pm tonight.*

When they were just arriving at the hotel, Patrick's phone buzzed again. This time a text message from Heidi with information on Sonrisa's flight out.

"It's at an airfield not far from the hotel," he said.

"If you can drop me off there, that would be great. I'll grab my things from the room."

They went upstairs together and Sonrisa was quiet as she packed her bag. Patrick wanted to say something, but he was at a loss. Should he tell her he hoped to see her again? Who knew if that would even be true?

When she was ready to go, Sonrisa faced him and cleared her throat. "Thank you for everything. I hope all goes well and you get to see your family soon."

Patrick nodded, the pent-up emotions in his chest making it difficult to speak. Finally, he said, "I wish you the best with Juan, and working things out with Toran."

"The words 'working things out' and 'Toran' don't generally go together, but I appreciate the sentiment."

Once at the airfield a few minutes later, he walked her to a small kiosk where she gave the attendant her name. The woman flagged down another employee, who quickly approached. "*Señora* Black," he said to her, smiling broadly. "We have your flight waiting." He took her bag. "Come with me."

Sonrisa turned to Patrick and embraced him. "Thank you again," she whispered. Then she followed the man toward a plane waiting on the tarmac.

As he watched her go, Patrick felt a lump form in his throat. Suddenly, a sense of foreboding came over him. He asked the attendant behind the desk. "Is that a private plane?"

The attendant nodded. "*Sí*, all of the planes here are private, *Señor*."

"Are there any government flights out of this airport?"

The woman shook her head.

Patrick's pulse started to race as the plane's engine began to whine. "Can you tell me whose plane the woman is getting on?"

"No, sorry, that isn't allowed."

Patrick pulled out some pesos. "I'm sure you could use some extra cash. I just want to know the owner's name, that's all. No one has to know."

He put his hand on the counter with the money underneath his palm and slid it toward her. She hesitated, then took the cash and began checking the computer. He prayed his suspicions were incorrect.

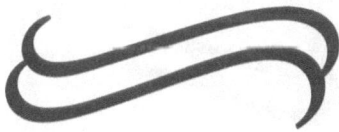

Sonrisa felt a tugging in her heart as she headed up the stairs to the plane. While she was overjoyed to know she would soon see Juan, she felt sad about leaving Patrick. Would she ever see him again?

A flight attendant greeted her when she boarded and pointed to a seat on the empty plane.

"Are there no other passengers?" Sonrisa asked.

The attendant, a man with short-cropped hair wearing a crisp flight attendant uniform, replied, "Just you and one other passenger. Please sit down, and I'll bring you a drink."

Just then the door to the cockpit opened, and she gasped.

"Andrea," Toran said, his eyes hard and bright with satisfaction. "At last, we are together again."

"The plane belongs to the Murray family," said the attendant to Patrick.

Patrick looked out the window to see the plane taxiing. "Can you tell me where the flight is headed?"

The woman frowned.

"Please. I promise, no one will ever know where I got the information."

She tapped a few more keys, her brow furrowing. "I'm sorry. I don't see a manifest."

Sonrisa found it hard to breathe as Toran came toward her. His good looks had faded over the last ten years, most likely from drinking. The square, strong jaw and dark green eyes that she once found so appealing made her recoil. "Where are you taking me?"

"Little Bird, asking too many questions, as usual. I'm taking you where I'm taking you. How's that?"

"Where's Callum? The American Embassy is expecting me to arrive in Scotland to get him."

Toran smiled. "It has all been arranged. You'll be reuniting with Callum. We both will. We'll be one big happy family, as they say in America."

Sonrisa didn't reply. She looked around the cabin.

"There is no way out, Little Bird. The plane is about to take off. Sit down."

Sonrisa felt a familiar helplessness slither over her as she took a seat.

The flight attendant approached then with a tray containing two glasses. He handed her one and the other to Toran. "Your favorite," said Toran. "Bordeaux."

Sonrisa eyed the purple liquid. "I'm not thirsty," she said, setting it on the tray beside her.

"Suit yourself," said Toran, who took a big drink of bourbon. Sonrisa nearly gagged at the odor, as it brought up so many unpleasant memories, like the last time he took advantage of her before she escaped.

Patrick returned to the hotel room and called Heidi Monroe, who picked up on the first ring. "Ms. Black?"

"This is Patrick, her friend," he said. "She left on a flight a little while ago. Did you arrange that flight? We received a text from you regarding it."

There was silence on the other end of the phone, then she replied, "I didn't send a text. My number must have been spoofed. I was just about to call her with the flight information. What flight?"

"It's the Murray family plane, and there was no manifest."

"Let me make some calls."

When Patrick hung up, he dialed another number.

"Andrea?" asked a man's voice.

"Andrea is gone. Taken by your brother. He picked her up in the family jet a half an hour ago."

"Who are you?"

"A concerned friend. I need to know what your brother is going to do with her."

When the man didn't answer, Patrick said, "I know you care about her. Tell me, so I can help her."

"Word is he went to our property in Belize."

"Does he have their son?"

"No, he's still here."

"She and the boy don't deserve any of this—you know that. Give me the location in Belize."

Evan gave him the address, then warned, "I hope you know what you're doing. Toran is lethal."

I can be just as lethal, thought Patrick.

Nick and Patrick ran for a good mile without stopping, finally arriving at Frankie's. Nick beat on the door, yelling for Frankie to open it. When he swung the door open, Frankie cried, "What the hell is all the racket about?" Then he heard sirens. "Shit, don't tell me you were caught." He pushed them both inside and slammed the door.

Nick rubbed his knuckles over his scalp. "I don't know what happened, Frankie, I swear."

Frankie looked at Patrick. "What the hell is he talking about? Did you get the notebook?"

"In his pocket," said Patrick.

"Well, hand it over," said Frankie.

Nick gave Frankie the notebook and money.

Frankie slid the money into his pocket and flipped open the book. "Woah, this is it! All the bigwigs in the city and what they've been up to. Good work!" He put the notebook on the bar and turned to Nick, who was sitting on the edge of the couch, rocking back and forth. "What the hell is your problem?"

"Nick shot the owner and another guy who drove up," said Patrick.

"What the fuck!" Frankie yelled.

Nick looked up at them. "The owner tried to take the gun, and the other guy was Paulo Ricci's cousin."

"Jesus H. Christ, you know what you done? You just started a war with the Brothers! And now the cops are going to be all over you."

"I can't go to jail, Frankie, I can't," said Nick.

Frankie ran his hands through his hair. "You both wore the ski masks, right?"

Nick nodded.

Frankie turned to Patrick and took him by the arms. "Confess to the shootings. I got a good lawyer. He can argue you were scared and confused, and you'll get out in a few years. Meantime, I'll make sure you're covered money-wise."

"You can't be serious," said Patrick, horrified at what the man was asking.

"I am serious," he said. "Don't do what I say, you and your family won't see the light of day tomorrow. You got me?"

Then Frankie turned to Nick and said, "We got to get your story straight."

As Frankie focused his attention on Nick, Patrick nabbed the notebook off the bar, stuck it in his pocket, and left.

Sonrisa struggled to contain the hysteria welling up inside. When Toran smirked at her, she turned away.

"If you behave yourself, Andrea, we can work this out."

Just then, the pilot announced they would be landing in thirty minutes.

"Work what out?"

Toran took another long drink, finishing off his glass. "Live together as a family. I'll allow you to be Callum's mother."

Sonrisa didn't reply. How dare he try to take over her and Juan's life, force them to live by his rules, like captives. That was never going to happen.

"A thank you would be in order right about now," he said, signaling the flight attendant to refill his glass. He leaned back in the chair, crossing his legs. "What do you say, Little Bird? Are you ready to let bygones be bygones, as they say? Callum is quite enjoying his new life, especially his pony."

Sonrisa couldn't bring herself to respond, a ball of resentment quickly growing in the pit of her stomach.

He laughed then, his eyes flashing malice. "Of course,

you'll need to share our bed with my girlfriends. But that won't be a problem, will it?"

Bile rose in Sonrisa's throat, but then she thought of Juan. "I'm sure I can get used to it," she lied, adding, "for Callum's sake."

"Bravo," he said, smiling wide. "We have an agreement, then."

"So where are we going?" said Sonrisa, trying to appear relaxed.

"Belize."

"Where is Callum?"

"He'll be coming along soon," said Toran. "I thought we'd spend a few days getting reacquainted first." He reached out to grab her face.

She jerked free of his grasp. "I want to see Callum first."

Toran scoffed, then got up and went to the cockpit.

Patrick paced the room, trying to figure out how to make both the drop and get to Belize that night. Maybe he could get an extension. He texted: *I have what you want, but I need extra time to deliver.* A return text came immediately. *We want it as planned, or you forfeit your chance to regain your life.*

He looked up the airfield they'd been at earlier and dialed the main number. "I'm wondering if you can connect me with anyone in the Yucatán area who does charter flights to Belize," Patrick said. The attendant gave him the name of a company, and he called immediately.

"This is Skip with S.S. Charters. How can I help you fly through the day?"

"Skip, I'm looking for someone to fly me to Belize tonight. I'm also going to need a driver when I get there."

"The latest I can fly out is eight pm," he said. "And it's going to cost you extra."

Patrick did the math. If nothing went wrong, he could make the drop and get to the airfield on time. He set up the flight, then texted them back. *I'll be there tonight, but I'm going to be in a hurry.*

An hour later, Patrick set out for the rendezvous. As he headed to a remote area in northern Yucatán, he hoped this was truly the end of the road and that he hadn't been stupid for trusting his unknown benefactors.

Patrick walked out of Frankie's apartment stunned. Go to jail for something he didn't do, but say he did it? It would kill his mother and sister. And what a horrible way for him to honor his father's legacy. Patrick stopped in the park and sat on a bench, his mind a rollercoaster. Frankie said he'd take care of his family financially, but could Patrick believe him? He had also promised Patrick no one would get hurt. Now two men had been shot and were probably dead.

He took out the notebook and flipped through the pages, peering at the writing in the light of the street lamps. Most names he didn't recognize, but there were a few, like the mayor, that he did. Frankie would be looking for this if he wasn't already. That thought in mind, Patrick got up and raced downtown.

The sun had set by the time Patrick arrived at the designated location, a remote area just off a main road. He parked the car and pulled out the gun, grateful that Estevan had shown him how to properly use it.

As the meeting time approached, Patrick became antsy. It was vital he be on his way to the airfield as soon as possible. The thought of Sonrisa alone with Toran, and the rage he must be harboring over her having left him, made Patrick gravely worried for her safety.

At precisely seven pm, a black sedan approached. Patrick sat up, taking a firm grasp of the gun. The car pulled up next to him, the windows tinted. Then the back side window opened slightly, and a slim hand wearing a black leather glove reached out. Holding the gun in one hand, Patrick handed over the medallion. The back window of the sedan closed, and the car sped off.

Patrick glanced at the clock on the dashboard. He had fifty-nine minutes to get to the airfield.

When the plane landed in Belize, Toran stood and grabbed Sonrisa by the arm, jerking her to her feet. He pulled her close, putting his hand on her bottom and squeezing so hard she flinched. Then he laughed and led her off the plane.

As they walked out into the balmy night, Sonrisa thought about Patrick. By now he had dropped off the medallion and would soon be reunited with his family.

"What are you thinking about, Andrea? Our time together all alone?" said Toran as they headed for the hangar.

"I'm thinking of Callum," she retorted, bitterness boiling in her at not seeing her son. "If you want us to be a family, why not send for him right now?"

A black limousine pulled up then, and a driver hopped out and opened the back door. Reluctantly, Sonrisa climbed in.

Once they were settled, Toran shook his head and tsked. "You took up your ridiculous painting again. That's how I found you. A little rag of a newspaper with a photo of you standing next to some atrocity you call art. Really, Andrea, why you bother, I don't know."

Sonrisa said nothing, but the fury at Toran's words continued to mount. She was a good artist. A great one, in fact. Francisco at the gallery and all the collectors she sold to attested to that. She realized as she listened to the insane ramblings of this man that he might not have changed—but she had. All those years ago, she had been young, vulnerable and naïve—but today she was a different person. Toran disgusted and revolted her, but she was amazed to find that she no longer feared him.

27

Patrick pushed the rental car to the limit as he tore through the Yucatán countryside. He checked the gas meter. He was getting low on fuel but there was no time to stop. At one point, a rabbit jumped into the road, and he swerved to miss it, almost crashing into the embankment. He shook his head to clear it. He had to keep moving forward and through. That was the only way.

As Patrick ran through the streets, his side aching, something told him that seconds mattered right now. When he saw the police station up ahead, he sprinted toward the doorway, then pushed his way through. He stood panting in the entryway when the police officer behind the front desk said, "Son, are you in trouble?"

Patrick nodded as he clasped his side and struggled to regain even breathing. "Yes, sir, I am. And so is my family."

"What does this involve? Do we need to send officers to your residence?"

Patrick approached the counter, the notebook firmly clasped in his hand. "This involves the Brothers and Mariano families, and yes, I think I might need the police at my house."

The officer picked up the phone. "I've got a kid here who has some information on the Brothers and Marianos." He hung up. "A detective will be right up."

Within a couple of minutes, a beefy guy wearing a white dress shirt, open at the collar, sleeves rolled up, approached. "I'm Detective Norton. You have some information? Come on back."

Patrick followed the officer to a desk, where the man indicated for him to sit down across from him. He looked at the notebook.

Patrick took a deep breath. "I made a big mistake, and two men were shot."

Detective Norton leaned forward. "Are you talking about the hits at the gas station a few minutes ago?"

"Yes, I was there."

"Did you shoot those men?"

"No, but I know who did. Frankie Mariano wants me to say it was me."

"What does that notebook have to do with all of this?"

Patrick handed it to the detective. "This is why those men got shot."

146

It was four minutes before eight when Patrick saw the airport in the distance. He put the gas pedal to the floor, willing the Hyundai to make it this last mile. He glanced at the gas gauge, he had to be on fumes by now. Just outside the airport entrance, the car started chugging. He pulled to the side of the road, got out, and ran toward the airfield.

When he was several yards away from a Cessna on the tarmac, the plane's engine fired up. He began waving his arms wildly, hoping to get the pilot's attention. The engine stopped, and a man opened the cockpit door and yelled out, "You Patrick? I thought you weren't going to make it."

Patrick came rushing up, struggling for breath. "My car ran out of gas aways back."

The man, who looked to be in his late thirties and wore his black hair in a ponytail, shook his head. "Wherever you're going, it must be important."

"Can you still take me?" asked Patrick.

The man waved toward the passenger side of the plane. "Get in."

Patrick climbed in, setting his backpack at his feet.

The pilot turned to Patrick. "I'm Skip. You said you have cash?"

Patrick reached into his pocket and pulled out the money.

After the man counted it, he put it in his pocket, then adjusted controls on the dashboard, and the engine roared to life again.

When they arrived at the house, Sonrisa was surprised to see that there weren't any security guards at the front gate.

Instead, Toran instructed the driver to get out of the limo and push the gates open so they could pass through. They drove down a dark drive flanked by palm trees and came to a stop in front of a low, sweeping building that was also dark. Where were the servants Toran usually had rushing around?

They got out of the car and Toran paid the driver, then the limo turned around and drove off. Toran headed up the stairs to the front door while Sonrisa stood at the foot of the stairs. Toran opened the door and said over his shoulder, "What are you waiting for? Come in."

Sonrisa glanced around the grounds and considered running, but where would she go? She took a deep breath and headed up the stairs. When she walked into the dim entryway, he slammed the door and gave her a look that sent a lump of ice into the pit of her stomach. She glanced into the nearby living room to see the furniture covered with sheeting. "How long since you've been here, Toran? The place looks unused."

"It is unused," he said. "We sold the place a month ago."

Sonrisa backed up, checking her peripheral vision for a way out. "You never planned on bringing Callum here, did you?" she said, spotting a dusty chalice on a nearby table.

"Did you really think I would let you have our son after you kept him from me for an entire decade?"

"What is your plan, Toran? To kill me here, then Callum will never know what happened to me?"

"Something like that," he said. "But first, we're going to make up for lost time." He reached for her, but Sonrisa lunged backward.

Toran laughed. "I've always liked it when you resist." When he advanced toward her again, Sonrisa grabbed the chalice, and with as much might as she could muster, hit him on the side of the head. He yowled and fell back, losing his footing, which gave her just enough time to rush up the nearby winding staircase.

"I'll get you for that, you little bitch!" he cried out, clambering up the stairs after her.

She went into the first room she came to, locking the door behind her. Toran began beating on it. "The more you resist, the harder I hit back," he yelled.

Sonrisa tried the light switch but there was no electricity. In the moonlight through the window she made out a dresser, which she pushed in front of the door just in time, as Toran managed to break the lock. She rushed to barricade the door with more furniture as Toran spewed the vilest words at her.

When they had been flying for a while, Skip said over the sound of the engine, "About another thirty minutes. Wish you could see this trip in the daylight. It's spectacular."

"How long have you been flying?" Patrick asked.

"Nearly all my life. My father was a farmer in North Dakota, so he used Cessnas for fertilizing crops. He taught me."

"May I ask if you're American Indian?" asked Patrick.

"Did my ponytail give me away?" Skip adjusted some controls. "My mother was Sioux."

The plane began to bump up and down then. "It always gets a little choppy in this area," he said. "Hang tight."

Sonrisa had put every piece of furniture she could move in front of the door. Despite numerous attempts to force his way in, Toran had failed, and was now crazed with rage. If he got ahold of her, Sonrisa had no doubt he would beat her until she was dead. Suddenly, it got quiet. She stood in the room listening. Had he passed out? She stayed that way for several minutes, frozen, her ears straining. Then she heard him on the stairs. What was he up to now? She ran to the windows and checked that they were locked, then peered out. The way up the building was steep.

When they landed at the airfield in Belize, Skip said, "I was able to set up a ride to your destination." He gestured to a car sitting in front of the hangar. "He'll take you there."

Patrick shook the man's hand. "Thank you. You have no idea how grateful I am."

"You take care now," he said.

Patrick got off the plane and hurried to the car. Once he was in the back seat, the driver said, "Mr. Skip gave me the directions. It will take ten minutes to get there."

Patrick nodded, praying that Sonrisa was still okay.

It was quiet for a time, but then Sonrisa heard a sound outside the doorway and Toran's voice. "If you insist on these obstacles, then I'm going to have to get rid of them," he said, his voice flat.

Sonrisa knew that tone of voice, and it sent slivers of apprehension up her spine.

"Let's talk, Toran. See how we can work things out."

"Too late for that," he said. Then she heard a clicking sound, and before long she smelled something burning.

"Toran," she screamed, and began pulling the furniture out of the way. "I smell smoke. Don't, Toran. Stop!"

"I'll burn this damn place down with you in it."

"I'll move the furniture," she said. "Then we can talk. You can believe me. Please, Toran, put it out."

He cried out then, making a shrill, animal-like sound. She reached over the remaining furniture and cracked the door to see Toran racing down the staircase, the arms of his shirt ablaze. Flames licked the walls in the hallway, and the fire, quickly becoming out of control, now blocked her escape. Running to the window, she pushed hard but it wouldn't budge. Behind her the fire had entered the room and was moving toward her, smoke filling the room. Sonrisa picked up a nearby table lamp and smashed it against the window glass. Then she leaned out the window and looked down the three stories to the ground as she gulped fresh air.

28

When the car stopped in front of a gate leading to a dark house, Patrick asked the driver, "Are you sure this is the place?"

"That's the address Mr. Skip gave me."

Patrick paid him, then got out of the car and headed to the gate, which he saw was slightly ajar. He pushed it open and passed through, checking the area for cameras, but it didn't look like anything was live. He took out the gun and started down the drive. After a few more steps, he smelled smoke. He looked at one of the windows and saw a figure. Could that be Sonrisa? He began moving quickly toward the house. If that was Sonrisa up there, she could be trapped. He ran around to the back of the property and saw a shed. Hopefully, he could find a ladder inside.

He tried the shed door, but it was locked. Just then, he heard shouting from inside the house, and the smell of burning wood became stronger. His only recourse was to shoot the padlock on the shed, which he did, knocking it loose. Then he kicked the door in.

Sonrisa couldn't see a way out of the three-story building without jumping. The fire would soon encroach farther into the room, and it would only be a matter of time before she burned alive. Maybe she could knot the sheets and get partway down and then jump. She ran to the bed and began tearing off sheets, tying them together.

When she had a length of sheets about eight feet long, she scooted the bed closer, then tied one end to the bedpost and threw the other end over the ledge. As she climbed onto the windowsill, a ladder thunked against the siding of the house. She watched as someone started up the rungs. He raised his head then. "Patrick!" she cried out.

"Get on the ladder!" he yelled. "Is Juan in there?"

"No!" cried Sonrisa, who turned around to find her footing on the ladder. She climbed down as quickly as she could, grasping the sides of the ladder tightly. When she was a few rungs from the ground, she felt Patrick's strong hands reaching around her waist.

Patrick was so intent on getting Sonrisa safely down the ladder that he didn't notice someone coming up behind them. Suddenly, he was pushed hard into the bushes. By the time Patrick was able to untangle himself and stand, he saw that his attacker had grabbed Sonrisa from behind. This had to be Toran. She was kicking, but he held her tightly. Patrick had dropped the gun when he'd been hit and now searched the bushes for it, but he couldn't find it. He noticed that Toran had been badly burned on his arms, but he kept his grip on Sonrisa.

Just then Sonrisa hit one of Toran's burned arms with her head. He immediately let go, shrieking in agony. It was then that Patrick saw the gun, now between Toran and Sonrisa. In a flash, Sonrisa lunged at it before Toran could get to it.

"You won't shoot me," Toran leered when she stood before him, the gun aimed at him. "You're too much of a coward."

"It's you who is a coward," said Sonrisa. "Hurting women. You call that being a man?"

"I didn't hurt you. You're just weak," he said.

"I have scars on my back to prove you hurt me, you animal."

Toran looked at Patrick then. "Who's to say it wasn't your boyfriend." He began walking toward Sonrisa, but she didn't back up.

"Come any closer, and I will shoot you," she said, her arms unmoving, her stance solid.

Toran stopped advancing as sirens sounded in the distance. "Stop this right now, Andrea, or I'll tell the police that you started the fire, and I came to stop you, but you threatened me with that gun."

The house began burning in earnest then, great clouds of smoke billowing into the air.

"If I were you, I'd be more concerned about yourself," she said. "Once all that alcohol wears off, you'll really be feeling those burns."

Toran looked down at his arms, then back at her. "Look what you've made me do," he said.

The sound of sirens stopped, then several police officers appeared at the back of the building, guns drawn.

Sonrisa laid the gun on the ground and put her hands up, and Patrick did the same. Toran, however, began moving toward her. When he did so, an officer cocked his gun, while another grabbed Toran from behind and restrained him.

An officer approached Sonrisa, who said, "You can check with Heidi Monroe at the American Embassy. I was kidnapped by that man, whose name is Toran Murray. He is a Scottish citizen." Then she gestured to Patrick with her head. "This man came to save me. It was Toran who lit the fire."

The firemen had arrived and were dousing the flames with a large hose. One of them called out that they needed to vacate the area. The police officer handcuffed Sonrisa and Patrick, then picked up Patrick's gun and led them away from the house. It took two officers to restrain Toran, who kept raving about Sonrisa trying to kill him.

The paramedics checked Sonrisa for smoke inhalation, then released her into police custody, while Toran was rushed to the hospital for treatment for his burns. They put Patrick and Sonrisa into separate vehicles and took them to the station.

An hour later, after the police questioned them both separately and spoke to Lance at Interpol and Heidi at the embassy, they released Sonrisa and Patrick, deeming them free of any wrongdoing.

"Mr. Murray will be charged with kidnapping and destruction of property here in Belize, and he will be charged in Scotland for kidnapping," the police chief informed them.

As they made their way out of the station, Sonrisa said to Patrick, "The good news is that even if Toran's father gets him out of the kidnapping charges at home, he still has to face justice here."

When they were standing outside on the sidewalk, Patrick handed Sonrisa the phone. "Did you want to call the embassy about Juan?"

When she hung up a few minutes later, Sonrisa was beaming. "Because of Toran getting arrested and the charges, the custody dispute is now void. Evan is going to bring Juan home to Veracruz right away."

"That's great news," said Patrick, taking Sonrisa in his arms.

They stood that way for some time in the quiet night that would before long turn to morning. "What about you?" asked Sonrisa. "Did you deliver the medallion?"

"I did," said Patrick.

Sonrisa's eyes searched his face. "So, it's safe for you to go home?"

Patrick glanced up at the sky, now turning a brighter shade of gray. "Yes, it should be safe."

"Can you tell me now what happened to you back in New Jersey that made you hide out in Puerto Vallarta all this time?"

29

Patrick wanted Sonrisa to know everything about him. He took one of her hands in his and said, "It looks like it's going to be a beautiful sunrise. Let's go to the park down the street, and I'll tell you all about it."

A few minutes later, they sat down overlooking a field of green grass. Patrick cleared his throat. "I got involved with organized crime when I was a teenager—with a New Jersey mob family. I was young and didn't realize what I'd become entangled in until it was too late. It started out with me doing errands, and the pay was good. But one night, I went on a run with the mob leader's cousin. We were supposed to rob a gas station, but two men died, including a rival mob member." He stopped and took a deep breath.

Sonrisa moved closer. "I'm listening. No judgment," she said quietly.

"I was so ashamed when I realized the part I played in the debacle. It turned out that our target that night wasn't money, though we did steal some. The owner of the gas station was holding a notebook in his safe for the leader of the biggest mob in the city. The guy I worked for was with a rival group of criminals. He wanted to steal the notebook, because he hoped having it would catapult him to the top mob position."

"What was in the notebook?"

"Names of people in the city taking bribes, including government officials. When we got back from the robbery, our boss, Frankie, wasn't thrilled that two men were shot and possibly dead and that his cousin had done the shooting. Frankie's solution was to order me to confess to the murders. If I didn't agree, he said he would kill my family."

"Oh, Patrick," said Sonrisa.

"I grabbed the notebook and ran straight to the cops with it. Fortunately, I talked to a cop who wasn't on the take. Several people in the precinct were in the notebook. I made a deal with the cop to tell him everything I knew about Frankie and his operation in exchange for not being charged for aiding and abetting during the robbery and shootings. I asked him for protection for me and my family, and he was honest with me. He said that the mob would seek vengeance for what I had done. That was a surety. The police could provide protection while the mob members were arrested and sentenced, but their reach goes much further than prison. The detective told me that my best bet was to disappear without my family knowing. So, I left that night."

"That must have been such a hard decision," said Sonrisa, who rubbed Patrick's arm. "Were you put in witness protection?"

"No, that's for defendants in high profile criminal trials. From the evidence in the notebook and my telling the detective everything I knew about Frankie's operation, they were able to make solid arrests, so there wouldn't be a need for me to testify. The detective set me up with a victim's advocate, who put me in contact with a network that helps people disappear. Having my family think I was missing or dead was the best way to keep them safe."

"And it worked?"

"It did. The detective kept his word to keep an eye on my family. He had an informant in the Mariano mob who reported back to him that they monitored my mom's and sister's phone conversations and social interactions for months after I disappeared. Because my family truly thought I was missing and feared I was dead, the mob became convinced they didn't know anything."

Patrick felt the dull ache in his heart he'd carried all these years since that night and grasped Sonrisa's hand more tightly. "It has been incredibly difficult to know my family thinks I'm dead. I figured I was going to have to stay away permanently, but then when the man from *La Causa* contacted me, I had a glimmer of hope. As I helped uncover the potential locations of artifacts, he kept insisting that the organization would eventually help me make my way home. Though I wasn't told the identities of those involved, he did explain their intent was to get the antiquities into museums before they were stolen by thieves and sold on the black market, which has become a huge problem in recent years. In fact, the man who attacked me that night at the pyramid was likely one of those thieves."

Patrick paused and shifted on the bench, noting that the sky was becoming a lemon color. "To be honest, I never thought going home was ever going to be possible, even with the help of *La Causa*. I was responsible for putting away some major players in the New Jersey mob scene. But then a few months ago, along with one of *La Causa's* requests, I got a newspaper clipping that talked about a string of mob members being killed. The victims happened to be all the people I put away. It occurred one day within a span of forty-five minutes. Some were still in jail and others had gotten out. I'm not sure who was responsible for the house cleaning, but when I saw they were all gone, I thought, maybe, just maybe, I can go home. Not long after that, my sister found me. I had called her once to let her know I was okay, and she never gave up hope on me."

"Cherie is going to be thrilled," said Sonrisa. "You should call her right now."

Patrick's face filled with joy as he held the phone away from his ear while his sister cheered. While Sonrisa was happy for Patrick, she felt a deep sadness knowing that they would soon be parting.

When he got off the phone, his smile bigger than she had ever seen it, he said, "She promised not to tell my mom and brother. I want to surprise them."

Then he frowned and looked like he was about to say something, but Sonrisa stood up suddenly and announced, "Let's get back to Veracruz. I have to prepare for Juan's homecoming, and you need to get a flight home." She forced a bright smile. "If we head out now, we'll be home by this afternoon."

Patrick had planned to talk to Sonrisa about the two of them, but when she jumped up and mentioned Juan's homecoming, he decided it wasn't the time. She was right. Reuniting with her son should take top priority. It was probably best to let her get back to her life, and he had a very anxious sister waiting at home for him.

Patrick and Sonrisa took a commercial flight from Belize to Veracruz and rented a car at the airport. They were back at Sonrisa's house by late afternoon.

He was just getting off the phone with the rental car company after sorting out the Hyundai he had abandoned in Yucatán when his phone rang. It was Cherie.

"I booked you a flight out of a private airstrip," she said. "The guy knows Justin and owes him a favor. But he's on a tight schedule and needs you there within the hour." His sister paused, then blurted out, "Please tell me you can make the flight. If I have to wait another day to see you, I'm going to implode."

After he agreed to get on the plane and hung up, Patrick looked at Sonrisa changing the sheets on Juan's bed.

She turned to meet his eyes. "You're going soon?"

"Yes, my sister arranged a flight to New Jersey for me."

Sonrisa hugged a pillow to her chest. "I'm sure she's thrilled about seeing you."

Though Patrick felt excited to see his family, a sense of loss washed through him about leaving Sonrisa. He walked over to her. It was now or never if he was going to tell her how he felt. Just then, someone rapped on the front door. Loretta's voice cried out, "Sonrisa! You there?"

"I should get that," said Sonrisa, hesitating.

Patrick nodded and went to gather his things. Then he stood back while both women caught up, until he had no time left. "It was nice to see you again," he told Loretta. He turned to Sonrisa, "I'll call you." Before she could reply, he walked out the door.

30

As she watched Patrick leave the house, Sonrisa tried to focus on what Loretta was saying, but everything in her wanted to run after his car and tell him how much he meant to her. She had to accept that he was anxious to see his family, though. They had waited and worried about him for a decade. Her thoughts returned to Juan then, with whom she'd soon be reunited.

It was late that night when a car's lights lit up the road in front of Sonrisa's house. She ran outside and down the drive as the vehicle stopped and Juan got out of the passenger seat. When he rushed to her, she grabbed him tight and started sobbing. Then she brushed his hair away from his eyes. "Let me look at you. Are you okay?"

Juan nodded vigorously. "I'm fine, Mom. Uncle Evan took good care of me, but I'm glad to be home."

Pulling Juan to her with one arm, she turned to see Evan standing in the drive. He had a beard now and looked older and more somber. But when their eyes met, he gave her the same understated smile she remembered as he said, "Andrea."

Sonrisa let go of Juan, who went running into the house, and faced Evan. "I go by Sonrisa now," she said. "Thank you for bringing Juan home. You're a good man, Evan."

"What my brother did wasn't right," he said.

Sonrisa smiled. "Come in, and I'll give you the necklace."

When they got into the house, she said, "It's in my art studio." Evan followed her into the room, where she slid her pottery wheel over and got on her hands and knees to open a door in the floor. Then she lifted out the display box and handed it to Evan.

"Father will be glad to have this back," he said. "The necklace's worth is quite great, but the sentimental value is even greater."

Sonrisa frowned. "I shouldn't have taken it all those years ago. I just wasn't thinking straight."

Evan studied her face. "I know you've been through an ordeal, but you look well."

Sonrisa laughed. "You were always so gracious with your compliments. Thank you. Can I offer you anything? Something to drink?"

Evan shook his head. "No, I'm going to head out soon."

"Now that Toran is facing charges, I imagine you are next in line to take over the family business?" she said.

Evan sighed. "There was a time when I would have given anything for that to happen, but now, I don't know." He glanced around the walls in Sonrisa's studio. "I always loved all your colorful art. It's so full of life."

After Evan said goodbye to Juan with a promise to do a video chat with him soon, Sonrisa walked him out.

"Thank you again, Evan, and take care of yourself," she said.

He nodded and turned to walk toward his car when Sonrisa said, "Wait! I'll be right back."

She went into her art studio and flipped through several canvases until she found the one she was looking for, then grabbed a padded box. When she went outside, Evan had just finished putting the necklace in his car. She kept the painting facing toward her as she approached him. "While my time in Scotland was difficult, I do have some fond memories," she said. Sonrisa turned around the painting of a moor at sunrise. "This is one of them."

Evan's eyes lit up. "That's lovely. It looks like the moor outside of the country house."

Sonrisa smiled. "It is. I want you to have it. I know how much you always enjoyed the view."

Evan took the painting from her. "I'll treasure it, Sonrisa. Thank you."

Patrick's plane touched down the next morning after a fourteen-hour flight that included a stop for refueling. He saw his sister jumping up and down on the tarmac, her boyfriend, Justin, by her side.

When Patrick got out of the plane and started walking toward her, she came barreling at him, nearly knocking him down as she hugged him. "It's you. It's really you!" she cried, covering his face with kisses. Then she turned to her boyfriend and exclaimed, "Justin, it's Patrick!"

Overwhelmed with a mixture of joy and relief, Patrick hugged his sister for a long time, then shook hands with Justin. "Nice to see you again," he said.

Cherie then marched him to their car. "I didn't tell Tad and Mom you're coming home, but I did tell them I have a huge surprise," she said, grinning.

When they pulled up to their family home a half hour later, Patrick felt tears at the back of his eyes. He didn't think he'd ever see the house again. A young man appeared on the doorstep, then he yelled back into the house, "Mom, Cherie is here with her surprise."

"Is that Tad?" Patrick asked.

"Yes," she said, opening the door of the car. They got out and stood on the curb. "Let me go first and give them a little warning. I don't want Mom passing out on the steps."

As Patrick trailed behind her, Cherie walked toward her little brother, calling out, "You and Mom should probably sit down for this."

At that moment, his mother appeared on the doorstep and met Patrick's eyes, her hand flying to her mouth. He walked, then ran to her. When they hugged, he felt her knees buckle, and he had to support her. Once recovered, she took his hands in hers while tears streamed down her cheeks. "It's you," she said, her voice thick with emotion. Her hair was spun with gray now, but her eyes were as warm and welcoming as ever. "My Patrick, I didn't think I'd ever see you again."

It took the next several hours to explain to his mother and brother what had occurred over the last decade. They weren't happy at first when they found out Cherie already knew Patrick was alive, but they came to understand it was for their own protection.

After a celebratory dinner of barbecued burgers and salad that evening, filled with a lot of catching up and multiple toasts to his return, Cherie and Justin left and Tad went to do homework.

When Patrick and his mother were sitting in the living

room alone, he said, "Mom, I can't begin to apologize for what I did."

His mother sighed. "I'm not going to lie and tell you the last ten years haven't been hell for me and your brother and sister, but I can only imagine how lonely it must have been for you. There was a lot of responsibility piled on you as a young boy to be the man of the house. I'm partially responsible for that. I'm just glad you are home. I sure hope you're going to tell me you can stay. We have so much catching up to do."

Patrick thought of Sonrisa.

His mother leaned forward on the couch. "What is it? We've had secrets for way too many years. Are you still in trouble?"

"From what the authorities here told me, I'm free and clear."

"Then what is it?"

"I met a woman in Veracruz." Patrick stopped, unsure of what else to say.

"And you care for her?"

Patrick looked at his mother. "We met under the wildest circumstances, and I haven't known her that long, but yes, I really care for her. She lives in Mexico, in Veracruz, with her son."

Patrick's mother smiled. "Have you told her how you feel?"

He shook his head. "There was so much going on, I didn't get a chance."

"Do you want my advice?"

"I would love your advice."

"This sort of chance might only come around once. If I were you, I'd tell her."

. . .

Two Months Later

When Sonrisa and Juan got back to their normal routine, she experienced a renewed energy and sense of purpose with her work. It was as if a waterfall of creativity poured through her now that she had completely broken free from Toran's influence.

Juan was especially excited about traveling to San Francisco to meet his Uncle Keith and grandparents, which they would be doing next month. Sonrisa was so happy to now be able to talk to her family.

At the same time, she felt a sense of loss about Patrick. He had said he would call her, but he hadn't. As the weeks wore on, she resolved herself to the fact that her time with him was becoming a sweet memory.

With all the new work she had created, Francisco insisted she have another solo show. "We need to get rid of some inventory to make way for your new masterpieces," he said. Now that she wasn't concerned about protecting her whereabouts, she let the gallery do a full media blitz on the show.

On opening night as she stood assessing a wall containing her various botanical pieces, Sonrisa felt someone walk up behind her and put a hand on her shoulder. She knew immediately who it was as she turned to face him. "Patrick," she managed to say, a mix of emotions overcoming her.

"I'm sorry. I know I said I would call you, and I started to call many times, but what I have to say, I need to say in person." He put his hands on her arms. "I love you, Sonrisa. I want you in my life, wherever that takes us. I'm hoping you feel the same. I want to be there for you and for Juan."

Sonrisa stepped toward him and buried her face against his chest. She looked up at him, tears in her eyes. "I love you, too, and I want to be with you. Is all worked out for you now? Are you free?"

Patrick looked over her shoulder then at the wall of her

paintings, his eyes registering surprise. "That yellow rose in a vase painting. When did you do that?"

Sonrisa turned around to look at the painting. "It was about two weeks ago. A man came into the gallery one day and talked to Francisco. He commissioned a painting of a yellow rose done by me. It was odd because he wanted it painted right away and paid well for the work, but then he never came to collect it."

"In answer to your question," said Patrick, his heart filling with so much happiness it took him a moment to finish his sentence, "yes, I'm finally free."

EPILOGUE

Sonrisa's and Patrick's stories are complete, but Skip Moore's is just beginning...

Skip Moore finished up his flight log and did a final check of his Cessna before heading out of the airport for the night. It wasn't hurricane season yet here in Acapulco but it would be soon. He made double sure the plane was secure after he tied it down.

It had been a long week flying, and he was ready to kick his feet up and drink a beer or three. He hoisted his bag onto one shoulder and headed toward his car.

He had walked only a few paces before someone came running across the tarmac toward him. He stopped, soon seeing it was a woman. She wore a black sweatshirt with a hood and a long, flowing skirt. "You have to help me," she said, stopping a few feet from him, out of breath. The woman was very pretty, with long, auburn hair and a beauty mark on one cheek.

"What's the problem?" He glanced around and didn't see anyone else. "If you're in trouble, you should call the police."

Terror raced across her face, and she shook her head. "Not the police."

Just what he didn't need—to be found with a fugitive. "Are you wanted by the police?"

"They're not after me for a crime. Please, can we take your plane?"

"Where?"

"Anywhere," she begged.

"I can't just take you anywhere. We need a manifest, a destination."

The woman suddenly pulled a gun out of her pocket and aimed it at his chest. "I was hoping not to have to use this. Get the plane ready for takeoff, now, or I'll shoot."

See what happens with Skip in *Discovered Promises*.

A NOTE FOR YOU

Dear Reading Gem,

Thanks for spending time with me, Sonrisa and Patrick! While each of the books in the Discovered Truth Series can be read as a standalone, it's fun to experience the progression and get to know the characters. The series progresses as minor characters introduced in each book become main characters in subsequent books. It's exciting to see what they'll do next!

The Discovered Truth series features complex, gutsy women and equally complicated, charismatic men who find themselves immersed in dangerous and intriguing modern-day challenges, such as human trafficking, drug smuggling, organ theft, national security threats, and identity theft. When the heroine and hero meet, worlds collide and sparks fly, kindling unforgettable romance and intrigue.

Thanks again and talk soon!

STAY ENLIGHTENED

Dear Reading Gem, thanks for reading! Let's stay in touch.

Join my weekly newsletter Julie's Reading Gems here. You get a free prequel novella to the series for signing up. There are also weekly giveaways and contests to win free books in the series.

You can also find me on my website at https://www. juliebawdendavis.com/fiction/fiction-books/the-discov ered-truth-series/, email me at Julie@JulieBawdenDavis.com, and follow me on Amazon.

Escape to Unforgettable Romance and Intrigue...

YOUR OPINION MATTERS

If you liked this book, please leave a review on Amazon, GoodReads, BookBub, or all three. If you don't wish to leave a review or don't have time, please leave a rating. Every star helps!

BOOKS IN THE DISCOVERED TRUTH SERIES

Discovered Beginnings:
(FREE at https://www.juliebawdendavis.com/fiction)
Discovered Secrets
Discovered Memories
Discovered Indiscretions
Discovered Liaisons
Discovered Betrayal
Discovered Denial
Discovered Distractions
Discovered Deception
Discovered Lies
Discovered Vengeance
Discovered Redemption
Discovered Obsession
Discovered Transgressions
Discovered Suspicion
Discovered Escape
Discovered Promises
Discovered Cover-Up

Box Sets

The Discovered Truth Series Box Set Books 1-4
The Discovered Truth Series Box Set Books 5-8
The Discovered Truth Series Box Set Books 9-12
The Discovered Truth Series Box Set Books 13-16